MORIBITO II

GUARDIAN OF THE DARKNESS

By Nahoko Uehashi | Translated by Cathy Hirano

ISBN-13: 978-0-545-10295-7

ISBN-10: 0-545-10295-2

Publication Date: May 2009
Format: Jacketed Hardcover Novel
Retail Price: $17.99 US / $22.99 CAN
Classification: Fantasy
Ages: 10 & up
Grades: 5 & up
LC number: 2008037444
Length: 272
Trim: 5 1/2 x 8 1/4

Arthur A. Levine Books

An Imprint of Scholatic Inc.
www.scholastic.com
557 Broadway, New York, NY 10012

For information, contact us at: tradepublicity@scholastic.com

MORIBITO II

GUARDIAN OF THE DARKNESS

NAHOKO UEHASHI

TRANSLATED BY CATHY HIRANO
ILLUSTRATED BY YUKO SHIMIZU

MORIBITO II

GUARDIAN OF THE DARKNESS

ARTHUR A. LEVINE BOOKS
AN IMPRINT OF SCHOLASTIC INC.

All rights reserved. Published by Arthur A. Levine Books, an imprint of Scholastic Inc., *Publishers since 1920*, by arrangement with Kaisei-Sha Publishing Co., Ltd. SCHOLASTIC and the LANTERN LOGO are trademarks and/or registered trademarks of Scholastic Inc.

No part of this publication may be reproduced, stored in a retrieval system, or transmitted in any form or by any means, electronic, mechanical, photocopying, recording, or otherwise, without written permission of the publisher. For information regarding permission, write to Scholastic Inc., Attention: Permissions Department, 557 Broadway, New York, NY 10012.

Library of Congress Cataloging-in-Publication Data

Uehashi, Nahoko.
  [Yami no Moribito. English]
  Moribito II : Guardian of the Darkness / by Nahoko Uehashi ; translated by Cathy Hirano ; illustrated by Yuko Shimizu.—1st ed.
    p. cm.
  Summary: The wandering female bodyguard Balsa returns to her native country of Kanbal, where she uncovers a conspiracy to frame her mentor and herself.
  ISBN 978-0-545-10295-7 (hardcover : alk. paper)
  [1. Fantasy.] I. Hirano, Cathy. II. Shimizu, Yuko, 1965—ill. III. Title.

PZ7.U277Mp 2009
[Fic]—dc22   2008037444

ISBN-13: 978-0-545-10295-7
ISBN-10: 0-545-10295-2

Book design by Phil Falco

10 9 8 7 6 5 4 3 2 1   09 10 11 12 13

Printed in the U.S.A.   23
First edition, May 2009

CONTENTS

PART I
INTO THE DARKNESS

CHAPTER I
THE GUARDIAN OF THE DARKNESS

Balsa stood on a rocky ledge beside a cave, the overlapping ridges of the Misty Blue Mountains dropping away beneath her. A stream rushed from the cave mouth and thundered into a basin far below, wrapping her in the tingling scent of fresh water. The hot, dry summer had passed, and the green foliage was beginning to fade. Within a month, the mountain slopes would be covered in a blaze of autumn leaves.

Balsa closed her eyes. The setting sun burned a red circle against her eyelids. She had stood on this shelf once before, after her foster father, Jiguro, had led her weeping through the caves. Just six years old, she had trembled to see the foreign land spread out below her; she could not begin to imagine the life that awaited her there. Years later, she was a bodyguard by trade, her black, weathered hair bound carelessly into a ponytail and her belongings slung over the end of her well-used spear. Those mountains to the south now separated her from everyone she loved in New Yogo, while to the north, through the cave, lay her native Kanbal, whose very name stirred bitter memories within her.

And yet now that was where she must go.

With her eyes still closed, she gently ran a finger over the long, twisting line carved into her spear shaft. *Right at the first branch. Right again at the second branch, left at the third* . . . She could hear Jiguro's deep voice reciting the route that the mark represented.

The rugged land of Kanbal followed the contours of the Yusa mountains, "the mother range," which hid a deep labyrinth of caves. Parents constantly warned their children to stay out of the caves, telling them stories of the darkness ruled by the Mountain King and the terrible *hyohlu* who guarded his kingdom. Despite these warnings, however, probably every child in Kanbal ventured a little way inside at least once in his or her life. While the rock near the surface was limestone, it soon gave way to smooth white *hakuma* stone. A piece of *hakuma* was the highest badge of courage among Kanbalese children, for it proved that the bearer had gone into the darkness beyond the reach of daylight. Every few years, one or two children who snuck into the caves failed to return. Perhaps they were eaten by the *hyohlu* as their parents claimed, or perhaps they simply lost their way in the complex maze of tunnels.

Balsa too had been taught to fear the caves, and though she had survived countless battles through strength and bravery alone, she felt the familiar terror rising in her stomach as she stood before the dark opening. She could have entered Kanbal through the official border gate like other travelers. Rogsam, the king of Kanbal who had hunted her for fifteen years, had died a decade ago. She was the only person alive who knew how he had seized the throne; she did not need to fear reprisal, even if she strode boldly across the border. But she wanted to return through this same cave. Somehow she felt that it was the right thing to do — to walk alone through the darkness, retracing her steps to her native land.

She had tried so hard to forget Kanbal. Thinking about it hurt like an old scar, tender to the touch. Physical wounds healed over time, but the more she tried to ignore the pain in her soul, the deeper it seemed to fester. There was only one way to deal with it: She must confront it head-on.

Opening her eyes, she took a deep breath, bidding a silent farewell to the Misty Blue Mountains and everyone she loved in New Yogo. Then she turned abruptly and stepped into the darkness.

Balsa walked along the stones close to the wall, carefully staying clear of the rushing stream. The light behind her dwindled to a tiny point and then vanished altogether, but she continued on slowly, her eyes open, keeping one hand on the wall. She knew that beneath her feet, the limestone of the surface rock would soon give way to the smooth white *hakuma* and eventually milky green *lyokuhaku*. Legend held that if a traveler went far enough into the cave, he might find the palace of the Mountain King, which was supposedly made of the most precious gem in Kanbal: *luisha*, the luminous blue stone. Balsa wished she could see her way now.

Never take light into the caves.

Jiguro's voice echoed in her mind. The memory was as fresh as if it had been yesterday, not years and years ago.

The hyohlu *hate fire. If you bring a torch or lantern, they'll smell it and track you down. The only way to get through here alive is to walk slowly, feeling the rock.*

Perhaps he had been trying, in his clumsy way, to comfort her, a little girl sobbing with fear.

Don't worry. I know the way.

As Balsa's feet and hands automatically searched a route through the darkness, her mind wandered back over the history that had taken her away from Kanbal. Jiguro had been a man of few words, very different from Balsa's father, Karuna, who had talked and laughed a lot. And yet the two men had been very close. Karuna had been the physician to Naguru, the king of Kanbal, while Jiguro served as the king's master of martial arts.

Ironically, this good fortune led to tragedy for them both. Naguru had always been sickly, and one winter he came down with a bad cold that lingered on into spring. His younger brother, the Crown Prince Rogsam, saw his chance. He ordered Karuna to poison the king. If Karuna refused or tried to reveal the plot, Rogsam said, he would kill the six-year-old Balsa.

Well aware of Rogsam's cruelty, Karuna was forced to do as he said. He asked him if he might use a poison that weakened the body slowly over time, so the courtiers would attribute Naguru's death to illness rather than murder. Rogsam agreed. He kept a close watch on Karuna until he began administering the poison, but as the king grew visibly weaker, he relaxed his vigilance. After all, Karuna could not possibly betray him now.

But Karuna knew the prince well, and he was sure that Rogsam would never let him live once the king was dead. Nor would he stop there: He would kill Balsa too to prevent future reprisals. In the time allowed him by Naguru's slow death, Karuna told Jiguro what had happened and begged him to save his daughter.

And Jiguro gave up everything — life as he had known it — to help his friend.

Balsa paused for a moment before moving on. Although she had been only six, her memory of the evening Jiguro took her away remained as clear and cold as crystal. It had been a warm night at the end of spring. The sweet scent of blossoms lingered on the air, and the trees and the stone wall encircling the house cast long shadows over the grass. Kanbalese houses were built of thick stone to protect against the long cruel winters, and Balsa loved to sit on the wide windowsill overlooking the garden. Karuna had not returned from the castle for several days, leaving Balsa at home with her nanny, and she had been waiting for him then, bare feet dangling out the window, hoping to catch sight of her father.

Suddenly she heard a dull thud, like two soft objects colliding. Startled, she looked toward the sound. She saw Jiguro opening the wooden gate into the yard, a bundle under his arm, and shivers ran through her when she realized the bundle was a man.

Jiguro looked at Balsa and raised a finger to his lips. The man was unconscious, and Jiguro swiftly laid him down against the garden wall in the shadow of some shrubs, bound him to a tree, and gagged him. When he gestured to Balsa to come down from her perch, she slipped quietly to the ground, moving as if in a dream.

Jiguro grasped her shoulder and whispered in her ear, "Your father told me to take you away from here. You must come with me right now."

She looked up at him. "But Nanny said it's almost dinnertime," she said. "I have to tell her where I'm going."

"You can't tell her anything. If she knows you've escaped with me, she could get in trouble. You see that man over there? He was waiting to kill you. If you don't want to die, you must do as I say."

He grabbed her hand and pulled her along after him. She began to weep silently. "My . . . my shoes," she whispered as they reached the gate.

"Ah, yes," he said. "I came prepared." He knelt and took a pair of shoes out of his knapsack. They were too big, but he laced them up tightly. "They'll have to do," he said as he stood up. Then, clutching her arm in his large hand, he all but dragged her out of the garden.

Years later, Balsa headed steadily deeper into the caves. She bit her lip as the memories came flooding back. From the time she had fled through this same darkness with Jiguro until Rogsam's death fifteen years later, her life had been hell. Six months after their escape, some migrant workers from Kanbal told them that Karuna had been murdered by thieves. It was a cruel blow, for the hope that she would one day see him again had kept the young Balsa going through months of fear and confusion. Jiguro told her everything then — why her father had been killed, why they had had to run. He spoke to her as if she were already grown up, and a terrible hatred toward Rogsam sprouted in her heart, becoming a hard knot buried deep inside her.

She had vowed to kill Rogsam, and she had begged Jiguro to teach her to fight. He shook his head. "Fighting is for men," he said. "No matter how hard you try, you're still a girl. You'll never have the muscle to amount to anything. And right now you're just a kid, so training could stunt your growth."

But she refused to give up. When Jiguro rose at dawn to practice, she rose with him and watched him intently, mimicking every move in his daily regimen of exercises. When he began working as a bodyguard for a rich merchant, she rushed to the scene of every scuffle and studied how he fought.

Then one day something terrible happened: One of Rogsam's hunters found them. While Balsa had watched Jiguro fight many times, she had never seen a battle as harrowing as that one. The two men appeared to be dancing — thrust, strike, parry, their spears whirling too fast for her eyes to follow. As his opponent's spear sliced across his shoulder, Jiguro's spear plunged through the other man's chest.

The smell of blood and the agony of death turned Balsa's legs to jelly. She could not move, even when she saw Jiguro crumple over his opponent as though he too were dying. But he was not dying. He sprawled across the dead man and wept soundlessly, his body heaving with sobs. It was the first time she had ever seen him cry.

It was not until much later that she learned why he grieved. The man Rogsam had sent to kill them was one of Jiguro's best friends. The king was not only powerful; he was also vicious. After this incident, Jiguro finally agreed to teach her to fight, for she would need combat skills if their pursuers ever killed him.

Balsa had thrown herself into practice with all she possessed, the thick, hot lump of hate erupting with every thrust of her spear and every jab of her fists. Although she was only eight, she fought like a mad thing, heedless of injury. "You're a born warrior," Jiguro muttered one day. "Perhaps you were fated to do this." His next words remained seared on her memory. "Conflict seems to follow those who learn to fight. If I could, I would spare you a life of bloodshed. But I have no choice."

Nor did he have any choice himself, for no matter how far they ran, Rogsam's assassins always found them. But Jiguro was strong — stronger than all of them. By the time Rogsam died, he had killed eight friends to save his own and Balsa's life.

Balsa was jolted back to the present by a change in the flow of air. She ran her hand along the rock wall, stretching out her arm until it ended abruptly and left her fingers swimming in space. She took a few careful steps forward, groping in the dark until her hand met stone on the other side. She had come to the first branch.

She checked the mark on her spear handle. She had copied it on impulse from Jiguro's spear when he died, not sure if she'd ever come back. *Even if I make a mistake, I can still find my way back as long as I remember how many turns I took and in which direction*, she reassured herself. She was beginning to regret her decision to come through the caves. *Perhaps it was just foolish pride, but there's nothing I can do about it now.* The longer she spent trapped in this thick, impenetrable darkness, the more she felt the air being squeezed out of her chest. She struggled to keep herself from bursting into a run. Besides the obvious foolishness of running blindly, her footsteps would echo deep into the caves, and if the *hyohlu* heard, she would never get out alive.

Moving carefully back until her hand touched the right wall, she turned the corner. The next turn would be on that side. *Right at the next branch, then left, and after that, left once again and I should be outside.* The rushing stream, which had roared continuously in her ears, gradually receded into the distance, and though her straw sandals muffled her footsteps, her breathing now seemed very loud in the silence.

She had just reached the next passage and was turning the corner when the acrid smell of smoke stung her nose. An image flashed into her mind: a midwinter's night, her father returning home through a blizzard, and in his hand, a torch that smelled just like this one, drenched in tallow to burn through the wind and snow.

A scream jerked her back to reality. The wordless wail bounced off the walls, echoing through the caves — a child's voice, high and shrill.

Dropping her bag on the ground, Balsa took her spear and sped cautiously through the dark. The crisscrossing caves distorted sound, making it hard to locate the scream's origin. At the next branch, however, she saw a light and raced toward it, taking care to remember the route back.

To eyes accustomed to the dark, the light of the torch seemed as bright as day, reflecting off the white *hakuma* stone with a brilliance that lit up the entire cavern. Then a streak of light whistled through the air and struck the torch, quenching its flame. Darkness returned, but not before the scene had imprinted itself on Balsa's mind: a boy gripping a torch, his back pressed against the wall, and a girl cowering on the ground beyond him.

The smoke from the extinguished torch tickled her nose as she felt her way to where she had seen the boy. His ragged breathing told her that he was still alive and, as she did not smell blood, she was fairly certain he was unharmed. Reaching his side, she grabbed his shoulder. He jumped. "Don't scream!" she whispered fiercely. "Tell me what happened."

"My sis — my sister . . . the *hyohlu* . . ."

Balsa turned in the direction of the little girl. Something lurked in the darkness just past her — something uncanny. Swinging her spear toward it, Balsa exhaled slowly. The stillness that always came before battle settled over her, and adrenaline surged through her veins, shrinking the world down to nothing but herself and the enemy before her. Drilled to fight even in the dark, she could just make out a phosphorescent pale blue glow. Keeping her eyes wide open, she shifted her gaze slightly to the side until she discerned a shape within the bluish haze. *So that's a* hyohlu, Balsa thought. She felt chilled to the core.

When she stepped forward, so did he. When she leveled her spear at him, he moved his toward her. It was like watching her reflection in a mirror. A deep, crackling tension bound them together and the heat of it flashed through her body. Energy rolled toward her, slamming into her chest like a wave crashing against the shore. She leapt toward him, but just before she drove her spear home, a shiver raced across her core. She jerked away quickly and a black wind grazed her side. Faster than thought, she knocked the *hyohlu's* spear aside with her own. Sparks flew at the impact, but already his rebounding spear was arcing down upon her head. Their weapons clashed with dizzying speed, thrusting, parrying, and whirling through the air like windmills. Balsa no longer relied on her eyes or even her conscious mind; her body moved automatically, waiting to the last possible second before knocking away her opponent's thrust and striking back.

A strange sensation crept over her. It was like she was dancing in a dream with her opponent as her partner, each move leading naturally to the next in the comfortable rhythm that controlled her body. Although their spears whined with ferocious speed, time seemed to move slowly, liquidly.

I've done this before, she thought in wonder, *a long time ago.* Indeed, there was something familiar about the *hyohlu*; he reminded her of someone she should have known. Their spears began to slow and the storm that had raged between them lessened, until finally they both came to perfect stillness.

Balsa exhaled a gust of air and realized with surprise that she had forgotten to breathe. Their duel, which had seemed so long, had lasted but a single breath! She thought she saw the *hyohlu* bow slightly, and she inclined her head in return. The dimly glowing figure receded into the darkness, and Balsa stared blankly after it.

What was *that?* she wondered. The encounter had been more like a wordless conversation than a desperate fight for her life. Once, long ago, when she had been practicing with Jiguro, their moves had matched so perfectly that they had fused into a single flow. "The Spear Dance!" Jiguro had murmured in disbelief. "So you've actually reached that level."

Balsa broke into a cold sweat. Was the apparition she had just faced not a *hyohlu* after all? Could it have been Jiguro? *Don't be ridiculous!* she chided herself. *He died six years ago. You buried him with your own hands.*

Just then she heard a faint moan behind her — the little girl. Balsa collected herself abruptly and turned around. Moving cautiously toward the sound, she reached out to touch the child. "It's all right now," she said. "The *hyohlu* has gone. Are you hurt?"

"My foot . . ." the girl answered between sobs.

Balsa felt the boy approach uncertainly. His hand, waving about in the dark, touched her head, and she took it to guide him toward the girl.

"Gina, are you all right?" he whispered.

"Kassa!" the girl cried.

"It's all right now," Balsa repeated quietly. "But let's get out of here. I'll carry your sister. Grab the end of my spear and follow me quietly."

The boy helped the girl climb up on Balsa's back. Recalling the route she had taken to find them, she traced her way back to the passage where she had left her bag. By the time they finally left the cave, the moon was already sinking in the west.

CHAPTER II
LUISHA, THE LUMINOUS BLUE STONE

Outside, the night air enveloped them, startlingly cold and smelling of snow: night's breath blowing down from the snowcapped mother range. White peaks glittered blue in the moonlight. Arrested by the familiar scent of her homeland, Balsa stopped and gazed up at the star-dusted sky.

"Er . . ." The boy looked up at Balsa, his face faintly lit by the moon. A head shorter than her but sturdily built, he looked about fourteen or fifteen. His tunic of tanned goat hide marked him as a member of the warrior class, as did the broad knife that hung from the back of his thick leather belt. "Thank you," he said, his voice husky, as if it had only recently changed.

"Yes, well, we were just lucky to get out of there alive," Balsa replied, and then added sternly, "How could you be so stupid? Taking your younger sister into the cave to test your courage! A young man like you with the right to carry a dagger — you should have known better. She could have been killed!"

The boy looked surprised. "No, you've got it all wrong!" his sister interjected. "I was the one who went in to get the stone, not my brother." Her voice was surprisingly firm and steady. Balsa had assumed she was only about ten, but she revised her estimate to twelve or even thirteen. "There's this boy in our village who's so stuck up — he keeps talking about how he's from the chieftain's line and laughing at us, and he said if *we* went into the caves to get a stone, we'd never come out alive because we're just from a branch family. That's why I did it."

Balsa suppressed a smile. "I see. Now I understand *why* you did it. But it still wasn't worth risking your life. You should never underestimate the caves. You almost died in there tonight."

The two children said nothing, most likely reliving the terror they felt when they met the *hyohlu*. The girl shuddered on Balsa's back, and she hitched her higher up. "Don't ever go into the caves again, you understand?" She felt the girl nod. "Good. That's settled then. Is your village near here?"

"Yes," the boy responded. "I'm Kassa, son of Tonno of the Musa clan. This is my sister Gina."

His words startled Balsa. Jiguro had belonged to the Musa clan. She had never heard the name Tonno, but still, it seemed a strange coincidence that the first people she should meet after twenty-five years were from Jiguro's clan. Now she understood how he had known these caves so well. This was his territory, and that was why he had chosen this escape route all those years ago.

"Excuse me, but are you a foreigner?" Kassa asked hesitantly, interrupting her thoughts.

"What?"

"You're dressed like someone from New Yogo, and the way you talk is, well . . ."

Since Jiguro's death, she had had few opportunities to speak Kanbalese, and she now found herself searching the past for words. Apparently they had noticed it too. "No, I was born in Kanbal. But I've been on a very long journey."

As she said this, her natural instinct for caution took over. She had come back to Kanbal to find Jiguro's family and tell them the truth about why he had to escape. But before she did that, she needed to know what people thought about their flight. Royal politics and treachery had forced them to flee; to reveal her identity too soon might be very dangerous.

She looked down at the boy. "You're Kassa and Gina, right? I want you to do me a favor." Kassa nodded. "Don't tell anyone that you met me in the caves. You can tell your family that you saved Gina yourself."

It was too dark to see clearly, but she thought that Kassa looked troubled. "Can't we tell our parents?" Gina asked from her perch on Balsa's back. "If you come with us, I know they'll want to meet you and have you stay for a meal. Please come with us."

"Thank you, but I can't." Balsa had already thought of her excuse for traveling around Kanbal, and she used it now. "I'm on a journey of penance to save my foster father's soul. If I accept any hospitality from your family, my good deed won't have any effect. You know that, don't you? So please don't tell anyone that I helped you."

The children nodded, and Balsa breathed a secret sigh of relief. The people of Kanbal believed that those who died without righting their wrongs suffered eternally as slaves of the Mountain King, the mysterious ruler of the land underground. Their only hope for salvation was for one of the living to abandon home and family and wander about doing good deeds in atonement for the dead person's sins.

Balsa had no idea if this was true. She had traveled widely and found that people's beliefs about where the soul went after death differed from one country to the next. She did not really care which of these versions was right: She would find out soon enough when she died. But people doing penance might wear a red headband or even don the clothes of the opposite sex, which would explain Balsa's spear and men's attire. It was the perfect excuse. *And besides,* she thought to herself, *it's not so far from the truth.*

"Can you make it home from here on your own?" she asked. Kassa nodded. "All right, then. Oh, and by the way, what did you do with the torch?"

"I still have it, but it was snuffed out." He held it up for Balsa to see. She frowned. The usually bristly top was flat and smooth, as if it had been sliced with a sharp blade. She remembered the whistling sound and the flash of light that struck the torch. Had the *hyohlu* thrown some kind of weapon? *If so,* she thought, *it must have been very sharp and broad. And even then, could he really have snuffed out a torch in one throw?*

But this was no time to be wondering. She lowered Gina to the ground and helped her climb onto Kassa's back, then took a flint box from her bag to light the torch. She gave it to Gina and asked Kassa, "Will this last you until you reach home?"

They nodded. She could see them clearly for the first time in the light of the torch. Kassa had a boyish face and looked a little unsure of himself, but she could tell he was a serious youth who cared about his sister. Gina was dark-skinned, and her braided hair was looped on top of her head. Although there was still a trace of fear in her eyes, her firmly set lips betrayed a strong will.

"Well, I guess it's time to say good-bye," Balsa said. "I don't suppose you could tell me the quickest way from here to the nearest market?"

"That would be Sula Lassal," Kassa said. "It's about thirty *lon* from here — what you'd call an hour's walk that way, down at the bottom of the valley. It's the biggest *lassal* in Musa territory, so you'll find lots of inns."

Balsa thanked him and headed down the path, but she had no intention of staying in an inn tonight. She would camp outside and wait until several hours after sunrise, when people were up and about. Then she would go to the market to buy some local clothes. If she wanted to be inconspicuous, everything else would have to wait.

The two children watched her disappear rapidly into the darkness before they set off for home.

"Kassa . . ." Gina whispered, "I'm really sorry."

He said nothing. *It's not something you can fix just by apologizing,* he thought. Still, he understood why Gina had gone into the caves, and the reason had a name: Shisheem.

"Let me tell you something," Shisheem had announced that day at school. "Warriors who don't belong to the chieftain's line aren't anything more than plain soldiers. They aren't real warriors at all. That's what my father says. I'm different, you see. I can be chosen as a King's Spear, like my father, and go under the mountain to meet the *hyohlu*." He looked down at Kassa and added, "We know the secret rituals, so we're worthy of such an honor. You'd die if you tried to enter the caves."

Before Kassa could respond, Gina said hotly, "Oh, really? And you think you wouldn't? All right then — prove it! Show us a piece of *hakuma*."

Shisheem smiled gently, clearly just humoring a child.

Then he put his hand into his tunic and pulled out a smooth, translucent white stone. "Here. See this? This is *hakuma*." He caressed it gently with his thumb. "Clan chieftains teach their sons the secrets when they turn fifteen. Of course I can't tell you what we do, but I've been training for over a year now. So you can dare me all you want — it's just stupid kid games to me."

His words seemed to reach Kassa from some far and lofty place. Kassa was one of the shortest boys in his clan and not particularly strong, but he made up for it by being a fast runner and a decent spear-wielder. While Shisheem was taller and stronger, Kassa could still hone his warrior skills through effort and perseverance.

But what Shisheem was talking about now was a completely different matter: There was nothing Kassa could do about his birth. The King's Spears were the highest-ranked warriors in Kanbal. They lived in the capital and acted as the king's shield and guard, his last wall of defense in the event of an attack. More importantly, they alone had the glorious honor of meeting the Mountain King in his underground palace, which was said to be made of luminous blue *luisha*.

But just as a commoner or a shepherd could never become a warrior, Kassa, though born to the warrior class, could never hope to become one of the nine Spears. Only direct descendants of the clan's founder could be chosen, and the right was passed from father to son. Youth from the chieftain's line went to live in the capital at the age of fifteen or sixteen, not long after they received their dagger, to devote themselves to acquiring the skills, etiquette, and knowledge required of upper-class warriors. Shisheem would likely leave for the capital soon, and one day he might even become a Spear. But Kassa would stay here in the village. Every winter he would migrate to New Yogo for work, and the rest of the year he would follow the goats with the Herder People, acting as their overlord. His skills as a warrior would only be called upon in the event of a war with another country.

Although Kassa envied Shisheem, in his heart he was resigned. But Gina was stubborn, and too young to have given up on the future. On the way home from school, she looked up at Kassa and said, "The chieftain's blood runs in our veins too, right?"

"Yes, Mother is the chieftain's younger sister," Kassa said automatically. "But warrior blood is passed from father to son. That means nothing."

"Kassa, you give up too easily!" Gina protested. "Even commoners bring back stones from the caves."

It's not bringing back a stone that's important, Kassa thought, but he didn't feel like explaining it to his sister. She fell silent, but he could guess what she was thinking.

"Don't do anything stupid, Gina."

She glared at him. "What do you mean by stupid?"

"I mean, don't even *think* about going into those caves to bring back a stone."

Before she could answer, some friends ran up and interrupted them. The rest of the day went by as usual, and Kassa forgot all about their conversation until he came home in the dark after spear practice.

Commoners in Kanbal lived in one-room houses of thick stone, with steep roofs to keep the snow off. As Kassa's family belonged to the warrior class, they had an attic, where he and Gina slept. It was the time of year when the nights grew longer and they ate just two meals a day, a late breakfast and an early dinner, to save their lamp oil. Gina had gone to bed right after supper — or at least she should have. But when Kassa saw a thick rope hanging down the outside wall from the smoke hole in the attic, he knew immediately what his sister had done.

He entered the house and, without telling his parents, went up to his room, pretending that he too was going to bed. Then he climbed down the rope and went after Gina. Before he left, he grabbed a torch from the toolshed. Then he ran all the way to the caves. As he was a fast runner, he fully expected to catch up with Gina, but he was not so lucky. By the light of his torch he could see her small footprints leading inside. He had to admire her courage; the caves were terrifying enough in the daytime. Even though she had chosen to go at night just to keep from getting caught, she was still the only girl he knew who would dare to set foot inside them after dark.

He stood anxiously at the mouth of the cave, hoping to

meet her on her way out. But no matter how long he waited, she did not appear, and he grew increasingly concerned. He was sure she would have gone slowly, feeling her way along the wall so that she would not get lost. But if so, then what could be taking her so long? Various possibilities passed through his head. Perhaps she needed time to dig out a stone, or maybe *hakuma* could only be found a long way inside. But there was another possibility that stuck in his mind and stayed there: the *hyohlu*.

Unable to stand the suspense any longer, he finally went inside. With the torch in his right hand, he ran his left hand along the wall and followed Gina's footprints in the rough sand. He was afraid to call her name in case the *hyohlu* heard. The

cave gradually broadened, and soon the light of the torch began reflecting off the glittering walls. *Hakuma!* For a second, he forgot about Gina and bent to pick up a stone lying at his feet. He stood there caressing it, marveling at its smoothness. Then he tucked it into his tunic. *Really, Shisheem!* he thought. *What was the big deal about that?* He smiled to himself.

Just then, he heard Gina scream. She sounded very close. He broke into a run, following her voice. He turned a corner and his blood froze. In the light of the torch, he saw Gina lying on the ground and a black shape towering over her.

Gina! He'll eat her! But he could not reach for his dagger. Fear had rooted him to the spot. He could not even scream.

Feeling the warmth of his sister on his back, Kassa silently thanked the woman they had met. But for her, he and Gina would be dead. He realized suddenly just how precious life was. Yet the fact that he had been unable to lift even a finger to save his sister stabbed him to the heart. *I guess it's true. I don't have what it takes to be a Spear.*

As if she had heard his thoughts, Gina suddenly blurted out, "You know, that proves it, Kassa. Shisheem's a liar."

"What?"

"That lady, she fought the *hyohlu* and saved us, didn't she? She's a woman, right? So that proves you don't have to be from the chieftain's line and you don't even have to be a man to beat the *hyohlu*."

Kassa stopped in his tracks. Gina was right. "Yes," he said, "but it could have been because she wasn't afraid of dying. She's doing penance, after all."

Gina laughed. "So what? It still shows that who your parents are or whether you're a girl or a boy have nothing to do with it. I can't wait to see Shisheem's face tomorrow!"

"Wait a minute! You can't tell Shisheem that you met her. We promised to keep it a secret." He started walking again.

"Oh, right," she said, disappointed. But then she began wriggling on his back.

"Cut that out! You're heavy enough as it is without squirming around."

Gina shoved her fist under his nose. "But look! I can still

get back at Shisheem! A piece of *hakuma* fell inside my tunic when the *hyohlu* got near me."

"Is that all?" Kassa started to say, planning to tell her about the piece he'd picked up himself. But a blue light was seeping out from between Gina's fingers, and he gasped instead.

She opened her hand to reveal the stone and gave a small squeak. It was not *hakuma* but *luisha*, the most precious gem in Kanbal.

CHAPTER III
AUNT YUKA'S HOUSE OF HEALING

Sula Lassal market lay at the bottom of a bowl-shaped valley. About thirty shops lined the crossroads where two main thoroughfares met. Despite Kassa's claim that it was the biggest market in Musa territory, to the well-traveled Balsa, it seemed surprisingly small. The shops were just simple stalls with thick stone walls, a thatch of straw, and tables laden with wares. She noticed that many sold goods from southern countries, like grain and candied fruit. The mountain slopes of Kanbal were too steep for farming, and the only crop that grew well was *gasha*, a kind of potato. To supplement the meager harvest, the king bought grain from warmer countries like New Yogo and Sangal, sold it wholesale to local merchants, and then made them sell it cheaply to the people.

When Balsa reached Sula Lassal, she felt painfully

conspicuous among all the shoppers from the Musa clan. Wherever she passed, people's eyes followed her. She was glad that she had walked all the way around the valley to enter the market from the side opposite the caves. In the middle of town, she finally found a stall selling clothes, all brightly colored to make it easier to spot anyone who got lost in the snow. Long leather boots lay stacked on the floor underneath the table, and a few *kahls*, thick cloaks of woven goat's hair, hung on the walls.

The shopkeeper, a tall man with a face like tanned leather, watched Balsa suspiciously as she looked through his wares. When he saw the clothes she had picked, his frown deepened. "Surely you don't want those? They're for men."

His speech instantly brought back memories of Balsa's nanny. She had had the same accent, the slightly slurred roll of common speech.

"But I want men's clothing. I'm on a journey of penance."

The man blinked in surprise. "Ah, I see." His forbidding expression softened slightly. "I'm sorry to hear that. And where was it you were coming from?"

The owners of the surrounding shops and even their customers were straining to hear their conversation. Balsa gave up any idea of being discreet and decided to supply just enough information to satisfy their curiosity.

"I came from New Yogo. I was born in Kanbal, but my foster father took me to Yogo when I was young, and that's where I grew up. He committed a crime in Yogo, so I decided to come back here to do penance. . . . But please don't ask me any more than that."

The shopkeeper waved his hand in front of his face hastily. "Ah, no, I wasn't meaning to pry! It's just that the mark on your spear there is like the chieftain's, and I was wondering how you might be related, considering that you're dressed like an outlander and all."

Balsa felt her pulse race. *Oh, blast!* It had never occurred to her that people could tell at a glance where she came from, just from the pattern on her spear. She feigned polite surprise. "Really? I didn't know there was another clan with a similar mark. Well, that's certainly interesting. But this spear is a memento of my father, and I don't think he belonged to the Musa clan. . . ."

"Is that so? Well then, I guess you're right. There must be other clans with the same design. But there I go prying . . . That outfit with the boots is fifty *nal*. I'll throw in the belt for free because you're doing penance, like."

Balsa took out some coins. "Do you take Yogo currency?"

"I sure do. Yogo merchants come to buy furs around this time of year. One piece of Yogo silver is worth a hundred *nal*."

The woman who owned the stall across the street yelled, "Hey there! Don't let him cheat you just 'cause you're doing penance, you hear? That should be a hundred and ten *nal*." The customers burst out laughing.

"I wasn't going to cheat her," the first shopkeeper retorted. "I just meant that that's the exchange rate for Yogo merchants in my shop!" He winked at Balsa. "So how about it? While you're at it, why not buy that wool cloak? I'll give you the lot for one piece of Yogo silver. If you've been gone a while, you might have forgotten, but the winters here come early, and the cold is enough to freeze the marrow in your very bones. This *kahl*, though, it's woven from Kanbal goat's wool. The natural oils in it keep off the rain and the bugs too."

Balsa smiled and said she would take it. She was richer than she had ever been in her life at the moment, thanks to her last job protecting a prince in New Yogo. His mother, the queen, had paid her enough to live comfortably for the next ten years. Although she had left most of the money in New Yogo with her old friend Tanda, she had brought enough to last her for at least a year.

"In return, though, would you exchange another silver piece for me?" she asked. "A hundred *nal* will do."

"Hang on. I'll have to see if I have enough." He rose and opened the box on which he had been sitting. He counted the money inside and exchanged the silver coin for copper *nal*.

"Thank you. There's one last thing I'd like to ask you."

"And what would that be?"

"Can you tell me how to get to Yonsa territory?"

The shopkeeper went to the back of the stall and brought out a sheet of thin leather. "This here's a map for traveling merchants. I'll let you have it for half a *nal*." Although very rough, it showed the major roads leading to the capital and all ten territories in Kanbal, and Balsa was grateful for it.

She paid the money and left the shop. She had not walked far when a delicious smell wafted through the air — deep-fried *losso*, a thin dough of grated *gasha* potato kneaded with plenty of *la*, or goat's butter, and stuffed with various ingredients. The savory smell made her stomach constrict with hunger. She bought a *losso* sweetened with *yukka* juice and another stuffed with goat's cheese and minced meat, as well as some *lakalle*, a drink brewed from fermented goat's milk, then sat down on a bench near a group of merchants who had already started on an early lunch. As she bit through the crisp outer crust of the *losso*, the taste of melted goat's cheese filled her mouth.

She looked up at the sky, pale blue and distant. Far above an eagle wheeled. She took a sip of *lakalle*, which was very refreshing in this dry climate. *I'll borrow a horse from a stable in Sula Lassal and leave today for Yonsa*, she thought.

She belonged to the Yonsa clan, but returning to her native village did not mean that any family would be there. Her mother had died when she was five, and she had no memory of her grandparents. The only person she remembered was Aunt Yuka, her father's younger sister. She had a vague image of her as a tall woman who came to visit after her mother died, bringing over hot meals or sweets. But from what Jiguro had said, she sounded like a remarkable person.

Balsa's father, Karuna, had been known at school for his keen intelligence and dexterity rather than for his combat skills. When he turned sixteen, he had decided to pursue higher studies in the capital and become a doctor. Yuka, who was even smarter, asked to follow the same path, and the chieftain gave her permission, probably because he recognized that she would be of more value to the clan as a doctor than as a housewife. When they completed their studies, Karuna stayed in the capital as the king's physician, while Yuka returned to practice medicine in Yonsa territory. Balsa intended to seek her out first to find out what had happened since her father's death.

The folds in the Yusa range marked the clan boundaries of Kanbal. Each clan numbered about five thousand people, who grazed goats on the rocky stretches beneath the mountain peaks and farmed the plateaus above the forested slopes. Clan settlements of about fifty families each lay scattered along these plateaus, surrounded by low stone walls. Major roads ran through the valleys where the markets were located.

From a stable in Sula Lassal, Balsa rented a shaggy, short-legged horse that looked hardy enough to weather the cold winter. After riding some distance, she found a spring in the woods where she bathed and changed into the clothes she had bought. They were stiff and heavy compared to the clothing worn in Yogo, but also much warmer, particularly the cloak. The cold had kept her awake most of last night: Tonight she should sleep very well.

She reached the border between Yonsa and Musa before nightfall. It was marked by two crude stone forts on either side of the road at the top of the mountain pass. Relations between the two clans were good, and the guards merely watched travelers pass through while they grazed their goats. They gave Balsa directions to the nearest inn, and that night she slept indoors for the first time in a long while. Used to wrapping herself up in a *shiruya* and sleeping on the floor by the hearth like the Yogoese, she found it strange to lie in a rough wooden bed against the wall under a heap of musty-smelling straw. She smiled to herself. *My birthplace feels like a foreign country to me.*

The next morning, she ate breakfast at the inn and then set out to find her aunt, who appeared to be well-known. The innkeeper told her that Yuka ran a house of healing in the valley near the chieftain's village, about an hour's journey from the inn. On the way, Balsa saw women harvesting *gasha* from the thin dry soil in small plots shored up by stone retaining walls. Once again she was struck by the poverty of her native land.

High up on the rock-covered slopes she could see little specks that must be goats, tended by the Herder People. Eagles soared overhead, looking for dead goats or their stray offspring. And towering over all loomed shining white peaks that brushed the heavens.

Balsa's lips stung, chapped by the strong, dry wind. She rode over a low hill and looked down into a wide, gently sloping valley. She could see the chieftain's hall perched on a rise to the north and, in the foreground, a market about the size of Sula Lassal. Set apart from both of these was a group of buildings surrounded by a low stone wall. That, she realized, must be her aunt's house of healing.

As she drew nearer, Balsa began to feel like she had seen this place before. Perhaps her father had brought her when she was very small. When she saw a branch of a *yukka* tree overhanging a black stone wall, she was suddenly sure of it. The tree was laden with red fruit, and birds flitted from branch to branch, chirping merrily. The sweet smell of ripe *yukka* drifted toward her on the wind. She dismounted and was gazing absently up at the branches when someone moved on the other side of the wooden gate. A short elderly man with a rake in his hand stood staring at her.

"Is this the house of healing?" Balsa asked.

He nodded. "Yes, it is. Are you ill?"

"No, I'm not a patient. I'd like to meet Mistress Yuka."

He looked doubtfully at Balsa's spear, as if unsure what to make of her, but at that moment, a plump, sturdy woman of about fifty appeared at the gate. Her salt-and-pepper hair was tied back, and she wore a soft woollen robe. Balsa

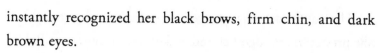

instantly recognized her black brows, firm chin, and dark brown eyes.

"I'm Yuka Yonsa. Did you wish to see me?" the woman said calmly.

Balsa's heart began to pound. All thought of caution vanished when she saw her aunt's face. "Aunt Yuka, it's me, Balsa. Karuna's daughter."

The woman looked at her strangely, as if she had difficulty understanding what Balsa said. Then her face grew stern, and she spoke quietly but forcefully. "Who are you, and why do you use my niece's name?"

Yuka had last seen Balsa when she was six. She could not be expected to find that child in the face of a woman already turned thirty. Balsa looked her straight in the eye and spoke equally calmly and deliberately. "I'm not using anyone else's name. I *am* Balsa."

Her aunt's eyes wavered. "But that's impossible! Balsa died when she was only six years old."

Balsa felt as if she had been punched in the chest. She had expected something like this, but hearing the words from her aunt's mouth still hurt.

"Did you see her body?" she asked gently.

Her aunt grew visibly paler. "No, how could I? She fell into an artesian well. She was swept away underground and —"

"Aunt Yuka," Balsa interrupted her abruptly, "you see the branch on this *yukka* tree? I don't know how old I was, but I remember falling from it and breaking my arm."

Her aunt's face turned chalk white, and her lips trembled. She pressed them together and looked searchingly into Balsa's face. With a shaking hand, she brushed back her hair. "Lusula, Goddess of Dreams," she murmured. "Is this a waking nightmare?"

CHAPTER IV
THE KING'S SPEARS

After much debate, Kassa and Gina finally decided to tell their parents about the stone. If they had just gone to the caves to test their courage, they could have kept silent as long as their absence went unnoticed. But *luisha* was another matter. A piece no bigger than a fingertip could buy enough grain to feed an entire clan for half a year. It was too big a secret for them to handle on their own.

They decided to wait until morning, as waking everyone up in the middle of the night would only make things worse. When they reached home, Kassa climbed up the rope first, then pulled Gina up after him because of her injured foot. They both slept little, nodding off only to start awake again, and greeted the dawn with relief. While they dreaded confessing to their parents, it was, as Gina said, better to get it over with.

When Gina came limping into the living room, her mother immediately noticed something was wrong. "What happened to your foot?" she demanded.

Gina glanced at Kassa. He turned to his father, who was about to leave for work. "Father, please wait. There's something we have to tell you."

When he began explaining their escapade, his mother looked stunned. "How could you be so stupid?" she cried, cutting him off. "You could have died!" She grabbed Gina by the shoulders, hugged her fiercely, and then smacked her smartly on the bottom.

"Leena, calm down," their father, Tonno, said, soothing her. He turned back to Kassa. "Go on. Tell us what happened next. You said that the *hyohlu*, the Guardian of the Darkness, bent over Gina?"

"Yes, and when I threw the torch at him, he ran away and . . ."

Tonno's eyes grew stern. Kassa's voice trailed away under his glare. "Kassa, do you really intend to lie to me?"

He turned to Gina for help but she just stood there looking deathly pale. They had promised to keep their encounter with the woman a secret, but Kassa could not lie to his father. The tale he and Gina had thought up last night sounded false even to his own ears. Finally he blurted out, "Well, no . . . We were actually rescued by a traveler on a journey of penance." The true story poured out of him. Tonno listened doubtfully, but when Gina pulled out the *luisha* and handed it to him, the blood drained from his face.

The stone's mystic beauty remained unchanged even in the light of day, glowing blue like the water at the bottom of a deep spring. The stone shone from Tonno's trembling hands, illuminating his face. Kassa's mother and grandmother caught their breath, mesmerized by the shining gem.

Gina broke the silence. "Father, does this mean we'll be rich?"

The adults glanced at each other for a second, then Tonno slowly shook his head. "Gina, *luisha* belongs to the king of Kanbal. You learned that at school, didn't you? It's not for people like us."

"But we risked our lives to get it! Can't we sell it secretly? To some foreign trader or something? Then you wouldn't have to go away to work in winter, and we could eat three meals a day all year round. . . ."

No one spoke. Even the adults, who knew full well that Gina's suggestion was impossible, could not help imagining what it would be like to sell the stone and make a fortune. Then Gina's mother sighed and shook her by the shoulder. "That's a foolish, shameful idea, Gina. Even if it could be done, it wouldn't make us happy. Just think about it. How would we explain our sudden good fortune to the rest of our clan? Even if they believed our lies, would you feel good about deceiving your own people and keeping such riches for yourself?"

Her words seemed to hang in the air, but their bitter reality was as heavy as stone. Tonno shook his head. "At any rate, this is too important to keep secret. We must take the *luisha* and consult Chief Kaguro. Kassa, wait for me after school. You must come with me and tell the chieftain what happened."

Kassa shuddered. He was afraid of the clan leader, a stern, forbidding old man who had lost his right eye and arm hunting a wolf one winter. "But Father, we promised we wouldn't tell anyone about the woman. She's doing penance."

"I have my doubts about that, and that's another reason I think we should tell the chieftain. Where did she come from? The darkness? And she led you out of the caves without once

losing her way? Can't you see what that means? Only the King's Spears, like Master Yuguro, should be able to do that. If she knows the caves in Musa territory that well, she may be a threat to our clan."

Kassa felt a chill creep over him. "But she saved our lives!" Gina exclaimed. "We can't break our promise to her."

"Calm down," Tonno replied. "I'm not saying that we'll do anything to harm her. But think carefully. What if she's involved in some kind of plot against the Musa?"

"Then she would have killed us both in the cave!" Gina retorted.

Well done, Gina, Kassa thought.

Tonno was momentarily at a loss, then he sighed. "I can't remain silent about something that could endanger our clan.

If she really was doing penance, then she won't come to any harm just because people know that she saved your lives. And if she lied to you, then telling the truth isn't betrayal."

Not even Gina could argue with that.

"Listen, I for one am very grateful to her. Even if it turns out that she *is* plotting against the clan, I'll stand by her to the end. Now are you satisfied?"

The two children nodded. They finished their breakfast without really noticing what they ate. As they left the house for school, Kassa suddenly realized that their parents had forgotten to scold them for entering the caves. The *luisha* had driven all that from their minds.

Little did he dream that, in the end, he would endure much worse than a scolding from his father.

Kassa had sparring practice that day. He took his spear down from the rack on the wall inside the school. Although its lethal point was sheathed and everyone wore neck guards of thick leather, it was far more exciting to practice with real spears than with plain wooden staffs, as the younger boys did.

Kassa clearly remembered the first time the sheathed tip of an opponent's spear had swung toward his neck: A shiver had shot from his throat to his stomach as he imagined, all too vividly, the point piercing his windpipe. Death had never felt so close.

He stepped out of the darkness of the school building

into the blinding sunshine, thin and autumnal despite its brilliance. "We'll have a practice tournament today," Muruzo announced. A big man of almost forty with broad shoulders and a loud voice, he was responsible for training the young men in the village. If any boy froze in his first encounter with a spear-wielding opponent, one gruff bellow from Muruzo was enough to break the spell.

There were eight fifteen-year-olds, including Kassa, and twelve sixteen-year-olds, including Shisheem. They broke into two teams of evenly mixed ages and lined up facing each other in two rows. Their shrill shouts echoed in the large outdoor sparring grounds.

Kassa liked spear fighting. An opponent with a long reach had the advantage when fighting with daggers, and Kassa, who was not as tall as his peers, always ended up frustrated because he could not get under his opponent's guard. With the spear, however, height and reach did not matter as long as one had skill. In fact, Kassa's nimbleness could give him an advantage over someone taller, as longer arms slowed down one's swing. Moving with a speed that bemused his opponents, Kassa felt like he was dancing in space. He won his first three matches and, in the fourth, came up against Shisheem. Looking up at the older boy, he remembered what Gina had said about him the previous night.

Shisheem smiled loftily. His confidence was justified, for he surpassed all his friends with the spear. He was, after all, the son of Yuguro, the chieftain's younger brother and one of the nine Spears. But few boys liked sparring with him, because he enjoyed toying with weaker opponents and defeating them in a flashy display of skill. Kassa especially disliked it because Shisheem always seemed to shove their difference in rank in his face. Today, however, Kassa felt strangely composed. From the moment they faced each other, he felt his mind grow calm and focused. The noises around him faded into nothingness.

Shisheem's eyes flashed. Suddenly, with a shout that split the air, he drove his spear mercilessly at Kassa's throat. Kassa instinctively raised his spear, deflecting the blow, and followed through, driving the point toward Shisheem's nose. Shisheem barely managed to twist away in time and blood spurted from his ear. The smile had been wiped from his lips and his face was white with fury. Leaping back, he leveled his spear again, and it whistled along the ground to flick up into Kassa's face. Kassa tried to turn the blow aside, but Shisheem shifted in the same direction, and the spear whipped back toward him. This time Kassa could not dodge the blow, and he felt hot pain sear his cheek.

"*Hold!*"

Sound returned with Muruzo's shout, as if an invisible curtain had been torn asunder. Kassa's friend Lalaka thumped him on the shoulder. "Good job! Nice work!" Kassa pressed his hand against his cheek and a smile touched his lips.

Shisheem was watching him. He put his hand to his ear and, when he saw blood, wiped it on his clothes. Some color returned to his pale face as he took a deep breath, then gave a twisted smile. "Well, Kassa, you've gotten pretty strong, haven't you?" He tapped him lightly on the shoulder as he passed. "You'll be a good spearman someday. Pity you weren't born to the chieftain's line. You'll waste all that talent herding goats for the rest of your life." He raised his hand to a friend and walked off toward his next match.

The excitement that had burned in Kassa but a moment before drained away.

At noon, he still had not shaken the gloom that weighed on his heart. His stomach growled with hunger as he sat on the steps, waiting for his father. He and Gina had just shared the cheese that his mother had given them for lunch, but it was nowhere near enough to keep him satisfied until supper. *If only we could sell the* luisha, he thought. Trying to cheer himself up, he let his imagination follow this train of thought. *I'd start off by treating myself to some grilled sanga beef with spicy* ganla *sauce. Then I'd buy a cheese* losso *with plenty of* yukka *fruit in the filling. . . .*

Still, he knew it could never happen; *luisha* was just too rare and too valuable. *Luisha* only came to the surface once every twenty years or so, when the flute of the Mountain King sounded from beneath the mountains. That was the invitation to the king of Kanbal to enter the land below, accompanied by his nine Spears and their attendants. There the Mountain King presented the Kanbalese king with *luisha* as a sign of their friendship.

According to the legend Kassa had learned, the practice had begun over a thousand years ago, when a brave young man ventured into the caves and found his way to a palace under the land. There he met a beautiful maiden with whom he fell in love. But she was the daughter of the Mountain King, and the king told the young man that if he wanted to marry her, he must best the king's son with the spear. Taking up the challenge, the young man defeated the *hyohlu*, the Guardian of the Darkness. The king praised the young man and let him take his daughter to the land under the sun. To make sure that both kingdoms prospered, he promised to send a gift to his daughter and her descendants every two decades. That gift was *luisha*.

The young man who wed the Mountain King's daughter was hailed as a hero aboveground. He became chieftain of his own clan and gathered the other nine clans together to form the kingdom of Kanbal. He vowed to use his right to the Mountain King's gift to care for all ten clans, establishing the royal custom of using *luisha* to purchase grain for the people. In return, the nine clans delivered *laga*, a cheese made from goat's milk, and dried meat from one hundred goats to the king, which he presented to the Mountain King in turn. The rites enacted at the Giving Ceremony were a secret known only to the king, his Spears, and their attendants; commoners knew nothing about what went on at the Last Door to the Mountain Deep. And yet a piece of *luisha* had come to Kassa. . . .

He saw his father approaching the school. As soon as he glimpsed his face, Kassa knew that Tonno was already regretting taking on this extra burden, and the thought filled him with sadness. When Kassa had turned fifteen this spring, he had been presented with his dagger and become a man, with the right to join the other men when they gathered at the meeting place. But there he saw a side of his father that he had never known existed. Tonno seemed so subservient, trying too hard to please the other men, completely different from the man Kassa had respected since he was a child — the competent overlord of the Herder People.

Reaching the bottom of the steps, Tonno looked up at him. He was wearing his best outfit rather than his usual torn and threadbare clothing, and he had clipped his dagger smartly to his belt and polished his boots until they gleamed. "Sorry to keep you waiting," he said. "Let's go."

Just then, they heard two shrill horn blasts from the village gate.

"Master Yuguro has returned!" Tonno exclaimed. A double horn blast always signaled the arrival of Shisheem's father, the second son in the chieftain's line. From his perch at the top of the stairs, Kassa saw a cloud of dust rising beyond the outer wall. Normally, Yuguro lived in the capital, where he served as the king's master of martial arts. Even among the Spears, he was considered the greatest warrior in the land, and he brought much honor to the Musa clan. People ran out of their homes and workplaces to meet him now.

A group of eighteen riders came first, hooves clattering on the white stone pavement, and they raised their hands in greeting as the people shouted, "Welcome back!" Yuguro followed on a magnificent black stallion of foreign breed. He held the reins in his left hand, while his right grasped a spear bound with the gold ring that marked him as one of the King's Spears. His eyes were keen in his hawklike face, his beard neatly trimmed, his body lean and fit. Despite a streak of white that ran through his jet-black hair, he looked much younger than his forty-one years. He exuded an aura of power coupled with a grace that drew people to him.

If my father was like that, I'd probably boast about it too, Kassa thought. Yet he could not imagine Shisheem ever being like Yuguro, no matter how many decades passed.

The gold ring on Yuguro's spear flashed in the sun as he approached. Kassa started, suddenly recalling the spear borne by the woman in the cave. He had only glimpsed it briefly in the light of the torch and paid no heed to it in his confusion. But now he realized that the mark on her spear shaft was the same as that on the spears of the chieftain's line. *Who* was *she?* he wondered again. The encounter seemed like a dream to him now.

The riders drew closer. When he caught sight of Kassa and his father, Yuguro smiled slightly and inclined his head. Tonno smiled broadly in return and bowed very low. Yuguro was always kind to his younger sister's husband, a fact that filled Kassa's heart with pleasure.

A young man right behind Yuguro flashed Kassa a quick smile — his cousin Kahm, the eldest son of Kaguro, the chieftain. He had just turned thirty-one this year. Kassa grinned back and bowed respectfully. Unlike Shisheem, Kahm had always treated him well, and Kassa, in return, loved this reserved, fair-minded cousin.

"Thank the gods in heaven," Tonno murmured. "The chieftain is an honest man but sometimes he can be very rigid. It's a relief to know that Master Yuguro will be there."

The riders galloped up the hill and passed through the gate into the inner enclosure. Kassa and his father waited until the dust from the horses' hooves had died down and then began walking toward the hall.

In Kanbal, the chieftain's hall was always in the middle of the village, on high ground surrounded by a stone wall as a last defense against attack. Once Kassa had looked down over a cliff at their village, and it reminded him of a boiled egg sliced in half. His house was located at the very edge of the egg white, against the outer wall, while the enclosure around the chieftain's hall was the yolk. The thought of boiled eggs now made his mouth water, despite his nervousness. While skirmishes had happened frequently during clan wars, the last century had been relatively peaceful, and the heavy, solid gate before the hall looked as if it was stuck open.

The chieftain's hall was a huge building made of smooth gray stone. The roof was shingled with thin blue-gray slates and steeply peaked so that the heavy snows would slide off in winter. An archers' gallery circled the top of the building just beneath the roof. At the guardhouse beside the entrance to the hall, Tonno told a young man that he had urgent news for the chieftain. The hall was in a flurry due to the arrival of Yuguro and Kahm, and it was some time before the young man returned and told them to enter.

Inside it was dim and chilly. Neither the few tallow candles placed in brackets along the walls nor the sun slanting through the small skylights could banish the shadows from the wide, high-ceilinged corridor. As he walked along the passageway, his boots echoing, Kassa could not help thinking how much warmer, brighter, and more comfortable his own home was.

The pungent smell of smoke assailed them as they entered the chieftain's chamber, which likewise felt cold and cavernous. There was a huge fireplace built into the north wall, but even in the middle of winter the chieftain would only permit a small blaze during the day.

Kaguro stood up from a large chair beside the fireplace. "Tonno. Kassa. Welcome," he said in a deep, rumbling voice. He had assumed the chieftainship at a young age due to his father's untimely death, and he bore himself with great dignity. But where his younger brother Yuguro was like the sun to Kassa, Kaguro seemed like the dark night. He had a beak-like nose and closely cropped gray hair and beard, and an ugly scar ran from his right eye to his chin, the mark of the wolf that had robbed him of his eye and arm.

Before Tonno could speak, they heard two raps on the door and Yuguro entered.

"Kaguro . . . Oh, Tonno. Sorry. Did I interrupt you?" he asked.

"Not at all, Master Yuguro," Tonno replied in an awed voice, looking back and forth between Yuguro and Kaguro. "I know how busy you must be, but if possible, there is a matter on which I wish to consult both of you. . . ."

Yuguro frowned for an instant, but then nodded cheerfully and closed the door behind him. Tonno began to speak nervously. He must have gone over the story many times in his mind. While he occasionally checked a detail or two with Kassa, his explanation was clear and succinct.

Kaguro and Yuguro listened, expressionless at first. But when they heard that an unknown woman had bested the *hyohlu* they began to frown, and by the time his father had finished, they were both looking at Kassa incredulously.

"Tonno, I know you mean well," Yuguro said with a smile, "but I'm afraid I can't believe your story. I can't help but think that Kassa made the whole thing up." He fixed a stern gaze on Kassa, as if to say, *You might fool your father, but you can't fool me.*

"Yes," Tonno replied. "That's what I thought at first too. Until I saw what the *hyohlu* had dropped when he bent over my daughter." He pulled out a cloth and unfolded it. A blue light shone from his hand.

The chieftain and his brother caught their breath. Yuguro walked over and picked up the stone. "It's *luisha!*"

The two brothers looked at each other for a long moment, then Kaguro returned his gaze to Kassa and his father. "If your tale is true, then there are a couple of points that puzzle me." He stared at them as though weighing something in his mind before speaking again. "What I'm about to tell you is known only to those belonging to the chieftain's line. But you are my younger sister's family: Will you vow not to tell anyone else?"

After Kassa and his father nervously promised to keep the secret, Kaguro continued. "First of all, it's unusual to see the *hyohlu* so close to the surface. Many people believe that children who disappear in the caves are eaten by the *hyohlu*, but we know that, in most cases, they simply get lost and can't get out again, or they're swept away by a stream and drown. The *hyohlu* are servants of the Mountain King. They would only harm someone from overland if that person wandered very deep into the caves and committed a great evil. Gina was probably so startled by the *hyohlu* that she stumbled and fell.

"But Kassa, you said that you took a torch into the caves, right?" Kassa nodded. "That was a very dangerous thing to do. The *hyohlu* hate fire, and they will try to extinguish a burning torch. Sometimes they inadvertently hurt or kill people in the process. If a *hyohlu* really did come up near the surface as you say — and I have no doubt that it did, if that stone fell off its body — then this may be the year the Gate to the Mountain Deep will open. If so, the king will issue his summons soon. But then our next puzzle is this traveler. You said she was a woman with a spear, right, Kassa?"

"Yes," he answered, his voice catching in his throat. The gleam in Kaguro's eye was terrifying.

"And she fought and beat the *hyohlu*?"

"Well, yes, but Gina and I couldn't actually see what was happening, because everything went pitch black when the torch went out. But I could hear them moving and their spears whistling through the air. . . . The only thing I saw was the glow of the *hyohlu* as it disappeared into the cave. Then the woman told us that it was all right."

"And she led you through the dark out of the cave?"

"Yes."

"She didn't ask you to light the torch while you were in the cave?"

"No. . . ."

Kaguro turned to look at Yuguro and frowned. "What's wrong?" he asked.

Yuguro looked stricken, his face white and frozen. He blinked and looked toward his brother. "Nothing. I'm a little tired from the journey. If you don't mind, I'll just borrow this chair." He sat down heavily. "Sorry. I must be getting old. You were saying?"

Kaguro turned his gaze back to Kassa. "You said that she wore strange clothes and spoke Kanbalese like a foreigner."

Kassa nodded, then he suddenly remembered the spear. "There's something else. I caught a glimpse of her spear in the light of the torch, and I just realized that the mark on it was the same as the one on Master Yuguro's spear."

Beads of sweat broke out on Kaguro's brow. He turned to his brother and muttered, "Could it be *his* spear?"

Yuguro stared at him without answering.

CHAPTER V
TREACHERY REVEALED

Aunt Yuka led Balsa into her living room and asked her to wait while she saw to some patients. Balsa sat down in a chair by the window. It was a comfortable room. The polished stone floor was strewn with sweet-smelling dried grasses, and a breeze bearing the scent of *yukka* fruit wafted through a window larger than those in most Kanbalese homes. Red embers glowed in the hearth, and a gleaming saucepan hung on the wall inside the wide inglenook fireplace. In the middle of the room stood a table covered in a thin green cloth. A single book lay on top of it. Bunches of herbs hung from the rafters in the ceiling, swaying in the breeze. They reminded Balsa suddenly of her good-natured friend Tanda, who was also a healer.

For some reason, my fate seems to be bound to healers. She smiled as she recalled his face. *Tanda,* she thought, *did I do*

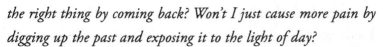

*the right thing by coming back? Won't I just cause more pain by
digging up the past and exposing it to the light of day?*

Fortunately, her aunt seemed to be as prudent as Jiguro
had said. Balsa would tell her everything. If it seemed wiser
to keep the past buried, she would leave Kanbal without
meeting Jiguro's family.

And never come back.

She heard footsteps approaching and looked toward the
door. Her aunt entered, bearing a tray with some baked
sweets and two handleless cups of *lakalle*. "Sorry to keep you
waiting," she said uncertainly. "Fortunately, there were fewer
patients than usual today. . . . Why don't you tell me your
story now? You can take your time."

Balsa took the cup her aunt offered. A hint of fragrant
spices filled her mouth with the first sip, stirring a memory
so familiar it made her nose sting with unshed tears. "I know
this flavor. My father used to give me this when I caught
a cold."

Yuka breathed in sharply. She stared at Balsa and nodded. "Really? Then perhaps you are Balsa after all. Karuna
and I developed this recipe when we were studying together
at the academy in the capital. It's made from a combination
of spices that warm the body, and it's an excellent cold rem-
edy." She sighed deeply. "Did someone rescue you after you
fell in the well and were swept away by the current?"

Balsa shook her head. "I never fell down a well. But before
I tell you my story, tell me what happened to my father."

Yuka looked at her with searching eyes. "My brother was killed ten days after . . . after you disappeared," she began. "The old serving woman found him lying slain at the back door when she went to work that morning. The palace guard claimed that it was the work of thieves. The house was a mess, as if a storm had passed through it."

Balsa closed her eyes briefly. Then she opened them and asked in a quiet voice, "Did you see his body?"

"Yes. I was staying in an inn in the capital because I was worried about Karuna. He was so despondent over your death. I wanted to stay at his house, but he absolutely refused, almost as if he knew that he would be attacked."

She seemed to make up her mind about something. Looking straight at Balsa, she said, "Yes, I saw my brother's body, and ever since I've wondered what really happened. He had two injuries. One was a deep slash that ran all the way from his left shoulder down across his stomach. Any robber who gave him a wound like that would have left him for dead. Yet they still cut his throat. When I saw that, I knew that whoever did it wasn't planning to rob him: They came to kill him. That last stab in the neck made absolutely sure that he was dead."

Balsa nodded. "Jiguro said that if you saw the body you would be sure to notice something wrong. And he feared it might put your life in danger."

"Jiguro?" Yuka said sharply. "You mean Jiguro Musa?"

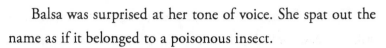

Balsa was surprised at her tone of voice. She spat out the name as if it belonged to a poisonous insect.

"Yes . . . Jiguro saved me. He raised me and helped me survive."

Her aunt looked shocked and confused. "You know, I still feel as though I'm caught in the middle of a bad dream. Your tale is like a twisted maze."

"Really?"

"Yes. Jiguro Musa was a fool, a complete idiot who caused terrible suffering to all of us from just plain stubbornness. I'd known him since we were children, and I felt so betrayed when I realized what a fool he was. It's true he had a stubborn streak even when he was young, but I never thought he'd do something like that."

Balsa sucked in her breath. "And what do you think he did?"

Her aunt's face turned hard. "If I'm going to tell you, I guess I had better start with what happened before that. You see, Jiguro and Prince Rogsam never got along. Everyone who lived in the castle knew that. Even though he was the youngest of the Spears, Jiguro displayed outstanding skill, and he was the best of the king's martial arts instructors as well. He never let the princes off easy, but worked them just as hard as everyone else. Prince Rogsam was older, and cunning too, but Jiguro frequently beat him soundly in practice. You could feel the hatred between them." She sighed.

"Prince Rogsam was a deceitful, despicable man. But still . . ." She looked at Balsa. "I don't know if you remember anything about succession in Kanbal, but the heir doesn't automatically succeed to the throne when the king dies. He must first be recognized by all nine of the King's Spears. Only when they pledge allegiance to him is he accepted as the rightful heir. At the coronation, all the Spears gather around and touch his head with their gold spear rings."

"Interesting. I didn't know that."

"Jiguro was considered a great hero. He was invited to attend the Giving Ceremony when he was sixteen, and all the Spears recognized him as the best warrior among them. Though he was a man of few words and never boasted, he did have a strong sense of pride. Once he made a decision, he never wavered." Balsa nodded. "That may be an admirable quality in a warrior," her aunt continued with a stern light in her eyes, "but the man who would bring misfortune on the heads of others for the sake of his own pride and stubbornness is nothing but a fool.

"When he learned that King Naguru was mortally ill, Jiguro stole the nine gold spear rings from deep inside the castle and fled the country. Those rings were priceless. They marked their bearers as the King's Spears and symbolized the bond that unites the nine clans with the royal family. The knowledge that Prince Rogsam would succeed to the throne would have been hard for him to accept. But to steal the rings and run away was unforgiveable.

"Only the king and the warrior clans knew of Jiguro's treason. We were all forbidden to speak of it because it threatened our ties to the royal family. After all, the common people could not be allowed to suspect any rift between the warrior clans and the king.

"To prove their loyalty to the royal family, every clan sent its best warrior after Jiguro. Before they left, these men took a vow of silence, pledging to Yoram, the god of thunder, that they would kill the traitor without talking to him.

"But Jiguro brutally murdered almost every one of them. Taguru, the eldest son of the Yonsa chieftain and our Spear, went after him too, but only his spearhead came back. He was such a cheerful, good-natured boy. . . ."

Balsa slowly brushed a stray lock of hair away from her cheek. She felt numb with shock. Twenty-four years had passed since Jiguro gave that spearhead to an itinerant Yonsa worker, asking him to take it to Kanbal and pray for the repose of his soul. "So he did as he was asked," she whispered.

She had expected people to hate Jiguro, but she had never imagined that he would be so cleverly transformed into an infamous traitor. Jiguro had been mistaken. His friends had not been forced to hunt him because their families had been taken hostage: They had done it to demonstrate their allegiance to the king and to protect their honor. Rage welled up inside her. She could not stand to see these lies so blatantly passed off as truth. How could Jiguro, or the men he had killed, or even her father ever rest in peace?

She stood up and looked out the window, then went to the door and checked the corridor to make sure that no one was there. Finally, she returned to her chair and looked steadily at her aunt. "Do you really believe that Jiguro was such a fool as that?" she asked in a low voice.

Her aunt's gaze wavered slightly. "I don't want to believe it, but the fact is that one day he just vanished from Kanbal without telling me or Karuna anything, even though we were his best friends. What else am I to think? I knew how much he hated Prince Rogsam."

"Jiguro was not that stupid," Balsa said quietly, still holding her aunt's gaze. "He raised me from the time I was six until I was twenty-four. I of all people should know he was not that kind of man. He was reserved — a man who did not explain the reasons for his actions — and he made decisions amazingly fast, but he was always considerate of the people around him."

Her aunt pressed her lips together firmly. Doubt showed in her eyes.

"It's true that Jiguro's spear had a gold ring. But only one. There were no others. Aunt, you and the people of Kanbal have been deceived."

"Deceived? By whom?"

"By Rogsam."

Her aunt's mouth twitched in surprise.

"Aunt Yuka, do you want to know why my father told you I was dead? Why Jiguro had to kill the best warriors from every clan? It involves royal politics, so if you don't want to know, it would be better that I didn't tell you."

Her aunt's eyes gleamed. "Is this plot still going on?"

"No. Once Rogsam died, there was no longer any point."

"I see . . . But even if it were, I suppose I would still want to know." She smiled slowly. "You were too young to have known, but Karuna, Jiguro, and I were great friends from the very first time we met in the capital. . . ."

Balsa tried to imagine what they had been like in their youth, before she was born. She could tell that her aunt was plainspoken and highly principled. The three of them would have gotten along very well. Then, one day, all of that had come crashing down. How had Yuka felt, Balsa wondered, when her best friend fled the country and her brother was murdered, leaving her all on her own?

She began telling the tale of Rogsam's treachery, speaking without emotion, yet all the while thinking about how one man's evil ambitions had warped so many lives. By the time she finished, twilight was creeping into the room.

Yuka gave a long sigh. "Ah. At last, the twisted threads have been untangled." She looked exhausted but, at the same time, deeply relieved, as if a thorn stuck in her heart for years had finally been removed. "I always wondered about my brother's death, but your story reminded me of several other things that bothered me.

"When King Naguru died, Karuna behaved very strangely. He was in such a hurry to bury the body, sealing it in a casket before other doctors could see it and insisting that it be interred immediately to prevent decay. It was unseasonably warm that day, so other people just accepted what he said. But I knew him well, and to me, it seemed unusual.

"I also wondered why Jiguro disappeared three days before the king passed away, almost as if he knew the king was going to die. And I couldn't understand why, even if he was planning to revolt, he would flee without telling Karuna and me the truth. . . . It seemed so out of character.

"Then the day after he disappeared, my brother told me you had drowned. So many strange things were happening — it seemed like heaven and earth had turned upside down! I had just decided to ask Karuna what on earth was going on when he was killed.

"Quite frankly, I was terrified at the sight of his body. I sensed some cold, evil will behind it . . . but it never occurred to me that it was Prince Rogsam." She broke off and looked at Balsa's spear. "Is that Jiguro's spear? I've been wondering ever since we met at the gate."

"No. Jiguro made this for me when I was ten. I've changed the head on it several times, but the shaft is so sturdy I've never had to replace it. When Jiguro died, I carved the mark from his spear onto it." She plucked the spear from the wall it rested against and handed it gently to her aunt. Yuka ran her hands along the smooth shaft, well oiled with use.

"It's much heavier than it looks," she murmured. "You started carrying this when you were just a little girl? Just ten?" She closed her eyes, and tears slid from beneath her lids. "What a cruel, cruel life . . ." she whispered. "Ah, Jiguro. How well you raised and protected Balsa. I can hardly believe it. To think a blunt and awkward man like you could have raised a little girl, all on your own. . . ."

Balsa felt her throat constrict and for a moment she was unable to speak. She had to breathe deeply several times before she finally managed to say, "You're right. There was never a man so unsuited to raising a girl as Jiguro. No wonder I have no idea how to be feminine."

Yuka chuckled and shook her head. "It's unfair to blame it all on Jiguro. You were a born tomboy who put the boys to shame. Karuna used to say you must have left something important behind in your mother's womb."

A single tear trickled down Balsa's cheek. The two women sat with their heads bowed in the dying light, chuckling through their tears.

Yuka wiped her eyes and handed the spear back to Balsa. "What are you going to do? Do you intend to clear Jiguro's name?"

Balsa caressed the well-worn shaft and sighed. Unburdening the story of her life seemed to have swept the dregs of grief from her heart. The fierce anger that had flared inside her earlier had died down to coals, buried beneath the ash of resignation. She smiled sadly. "What can I do? Even if I wanted to take revenge, Rogsam is dead, and frankly, I don't see much point in dredging up that plot now. I came back to heal an old hurt that I had been too afraid to confront. That's all. . . ."

Dusk cast a deep shadow on Balsa's face, and though she smiled, Yuka thought she glimpsed the darkness that lay over her heart. Jiguro's face rose into her mind, and she felt a cold stillness deep within. Though blunt, Jiguro had been kind. If he had been on his own, he would have returned to Kanbal and confronted King Rogsam. But he had been with Balsa — a defenseless little girl — and so his closest friends had come, one after another, to kill him. What agony he must have suffered when he fought them. And Balsa had seen it all. She had spent her childhood watching him slay his friends, one by one, for her sake. *What a hard, cruel life she must have endured.* Yuka clenched her fists.

As if she knew what her aunt was thinking, Balsa began to speak lightly and cheerfully: "Last fall, I was hired to guard a boy who had to bear a strange fate." She explained how she had protected Chagum, the Second Prince of New Yogo and the guardian of a water spirit's egg. Her heart filled with motherly affection when she thought of him. "The funny thing is," she concluded, "I was happy protecting him, even though it was an extremely dangerous and frightening job. I really was happy! And I realized that it wasn't such a bad way to live." She smiled slightly and took a deep breath. "Until then, I never really cared how I lived my life. It was just a miracle I had survived at all . . . a miracle bought with the blood of many other lives. I thought it was wrong to dream of the future.

"But Chagum helped me see my own stupidity. Jiguro will never be able to rest in peace if I think like that. He fought so hard to give me this life. The least I can do is enjoy and appreciate it." She laughed. "But you know what? I couldn't. I felt like there was something I still needed to do, as if I had forgotten to repay a debt. That's why I came back. If I found anyone among his friends and relatives who cared about what had happened to him, I was going to tell them the true story. I would bring the tale of Jiguro, who vanished so abruptly from Kanbal, back to where it began, and end it here. I thought that then his ghost would be laid to rest."

The room was now so dim she could barely make out her aunt's face. Yuka stood up and went to stir the dwindling embers while Balsa closed the window. The space grew brighter as Yuka walked around lighting the tallow candles. Then she turned to look at Balsa.

"Now I understand why you came back. I feel like I've lived through twenty-five years in a single day." They smiled at each other. "We haven't run out of things to say, but I for one am hungry. Can you give me a hand? We'll make some supper."

Yuka had no servants other than the gardener and an assistant healer. She told Balsa that living on her own suited her. Together they made a pot of *laroo*, meat and *gasha* stewed in milk and seasoned with fragrant herbs. The piping-hot stew was delicious, especially now that the bitter chill of evening had fallen.

As they lingered over the table, Yuka resumed their conversation. "I understand how you feel about laying ghosts to rest, but I doubt that any of Jiguro's relatives care what happened to him. His parents died before he fled the country, and his sister was probably too young to remember. As for his older brother, Kaguro, and his younger brother, Yuguro —" She paused suddenly and looked up at Balsa. "That's strange."

"What?"

Her aunt frowned. "If Jiguro didn't steal the gold rings, then how could Yuguro Musa . . ." She laid down her spoon and looked intently at Balsa. "You said that Jiguro died of an illness. Are you sure?"

"Yes. I watched him breathe his last. My friend Tanda was there too."

"And the illness wasn't caused by wounds he suffered while fighting Yuguro?"

"Yuguro? No." Balsa did indeed remember a man called Yuguro visiting Jiguro, but he had not been one of those who had hunted them.

Yuka looked troubled. "But that can't be! I told you that young men from eight different clans went after Jiguro and were killed by him. But the last one to hunt him was Jiguro's younger brother, Yuguro, from the Musa clan. He defeated Jiguro and returned with all nine spear rings. He's now the hero of Kanbal and wields tremendous influence over all the clans."

She pondered this for a moment and then continued. "Now that I think of it, many strange things happened the year Yuguro Musa came back. King Rogsam was found to have a fatal illness that very spring, and he insisted that his son, Prince Radalle, should succeed to the throne instead of Rogsam's younger brother. Yuguro returned with the rings only a month before Rogsam died. There was a magnificent ceremony; I remember it well. King Rogsam took the hands of his son and the hero Yuguro, and declared that a new bond had been forged between the nine clans and the royal family."

She looked into Balsa's eyes and whispered, "Could the plot have run deeper than you thought?"

Suddenly the room felt very cold.

PART 2
THE ADVANCING DARKNESS

CHAPTER I
THE SMELL OF STONES

Kassa and Gina smiled at each other as they strolled through Sula Lassal with their friends Lalaka and Yossa. Having just stuffed themselves with freshly fried *losso*, they were now sucking on delicious candied fruit. But more than the food, it was being able to treat their friends that made them feel so good.

"*Luisha* is the treasure of the king of Kanbal," the chieftain had told Tonno and Kassa when they finished relating their story. "Only he has the authority to sell it." And he had given the stone to Yuguro with instructions to take it to the king.

Kassa had known that he was right, but it still hurt to see him take it away. As if Yuguro had read his mind, he asked them to wait. He returned shortly with a heavy sack full of silver coins and placed it in Tonno's hands. "I know it can't compare with the true value of *luisha*," he said, "but let me give you three thousand *nal* as a payment. This priceless information could save our clan."

Tonno looked stunned. It was a huge sum of money, enough to feed his family for two years.

"Now here's what you should do," Yuguro continued. "Tell everyone that Gina and Kassa found a piece of *lyoku-haku* in the river and brought it to me. Although it's unusual, it does happen sometimes, and one stone would be worth about three thousand *nal*. No one will doubt your story — they'll think you just happened to get lucky." Then he fixed his piercing gaze on both of them. "But you must promise me one thing: Don't tell anyone about the *luisha* or the traveler. And make the rest of your family promise too."

Tonno and Kassa agreed. The reward was an amazing piece of good fortune. "I won't have to go away to work this winter!" Tonno yelled as soon as they reached home. Joy lit the faces of Kassa's mother and grandmother, and they talked late into the night about how to spend the money. Then Tonno gave Kassa and Gina two hundred *nal* each, along with a lecture about not wasting it. As one *nal* was enough to buy twenty *losso*, they could hardly believe their luck.

Gina was disappointed by the restrictions on their story. She had been looking forward to Shisheem's reaction when she showed him the *hakuma*. But she soon hit upon another plan. "I know! All I have to do is say that I went into the cave on a different night. I'll wait till things have settled down a bit, and then I'll make him pay for teasing us!"

As they walked through the village, Kassa decided to buy some *losso* for the Herder People who worked for his family. Warriors like Shisheem who belonged to the chieftain's line rarely had any dealings with these little people: They paid them milk and wool for looking after their goats, but that was all. Warriors like Kassa who belonged to branch lines, however, grew up with them as if they were part of the family.

Of course, there were clear distinctions between the warriors and the Herders. The Herders worked for the warriors, not the other way around. They never went to school, and they never married warriors or even commoners. They remained Herders all their lives. But Kassa spent most of his time with them after school, tending goats on the crags. Likewise, Gina and his mother worked with Herder women and girls weaving woollen cloth and tilling the fields — jobs his mother far preferred to spending time with her brothers' wives. In fact, she was so active and vivacious that Kassa suspected she had been just like Gina when she was a girl.

Before they left Sula Lassal, he and Gina each bought a bag of thirty freshly made *losso.* Now that their initial excitement had died down, they were anxious to escape from the marketplace. News of their good fortune had spread quickly and shopkeepers called out to them wherever they went.

"Wouldn't your mother enjoy some of these fresh spices?"

"Gina! Kassa! Come see what I have here!"

After parting from Gina and their friends, Kassa began climbing the steep, rocky slope. The clear autumn air bore a faint hint of snow. The higher he climbed, the more the world around him expanded. He gazed down at the land, which rolled far into the distance like waves on the sea, and marveled at what a beautiful world the god Yoram had made. The story of the creation ran through his mind.

In the beginning, there had been only whirling darkness. From this burst the first flash of light — Yoram, the god of thunder, or the "Backless One." The front of his body was the Great Light, while his back was the Great Darkness. He was the god of both the blinding thunderbolt and of the darkness from which it emerged. The ancestors who founded the nine clans were born from the body of the Great Light: from his right and left ears, Musa and Yonsa; from his right and left eyes, Muro and Yonro; from his right and left hands, Muga and Yonga; from his right and left feet, Muto and Yonto; and from his nose, Na. Kanbal, the ancestor of the royal line, was born last of all, emerging from the god's forehead. It was he who established the kingdom of Kanbal over the Yusa range. The Great Darkness likewise birthed children who founded nine other clans, and the line of kings that ruled the Mountain Kingdom beneath the Yusa range.

Each of the ten clans of Kanbal received their own territory and traveled to it. From afar, they saw only rocky mountains; not a blade of grass, not a tree nor a drop of water blessed the land. But when the clan founders set foot on the territory given to them, grass and trees sprouted from the soil, springs and streams flowed forth, and little people and goats emerged from the ground. The little people were the Herders, who cared for the goats and gave their milk to the clan founders. In return, the founders vowed to protect the land and the Herder People from harm.

This story always made Kassa wonder how merchants and tradesmen had come into being. Physically, they were clearly of the same race as he, so when, he wondered, had the clans split into warriors and commoners?

Suddenly he heard a piercing whistle. He looked up quickly and saw a Herder youth poking his head out from behind a rock. It was Yoyo, a boy he had known since childhood. Although Kassa, to his chagrin, was the shortest of his peers, he always felt like a giant when he was with the Herders. Yoyo was fifteen, like Kassa, but he only came up to his friend's chest, and even the adults reached no higher than Kassa's shoulders.

The Herders were a dark-skinned people with bushy gray hair and wide, lively eyes that animated their friendly, broad-nosed faces. They were very tough and wore nothing but leather breeches, except in the middle of winter. The soles of their feet were so hard they could run about the craggy slopes barefoot, and they were as nimble as the mountain goats they tended. The men always carried "eagle chasers," slender wooden staffs tipped with stone points, to fend off eagles that attacked the baby goats. Kassa had once offered to buy Yoyo an iron tip for his staff, but Yoyo refused, saying he hated the smell of iron.

"You smell good!" Yoyo called out to him now.

Kassa grinned and raised the bag he carried. "I bought thirty *losso* so you can share them with everyone."

Yoyo's eyes grew round with surprise and he swallowed loudly. "Wow! Thanks! It's just about time for a break anyway. Let's go down to Spring Hollow and meet the others." He let out a series of shrill whistles: *"Hiyu, hyo, hyo, hiyuwee!"* The sound bounced off the cliffs and multiplied. The Herder People could carry on an entire conversation in whistles alone.

Spring Hollow was a thicket surrounding a spring that flowed from a hollow in a rock. By the time Kassa and Yoyo pushed their way through the bushes, four or five other Herders had already gathered there, sitting about and chewing on *nyokki*, a tree root. Yoyo's father and grandfather were heating up goat's milk over a fireplace made of three flat stones. Toto, the oldest Herder male in Musa territory and a clan elder, was there too.

"Grandpa, Kassa bought us thirty *losso*!"

The men exclaimed at the gift. Yoyo's father added fragrant *koluka* leaves to the hot *la* to make *lakoluka*, a milky tea, and poured it into bowls. Then they divided up the *losso* and sat down to enjoy the feast. When they asked him how he had become so wealthy, Kassa repeated what Yuguro had told him. Although he hated lying to his friends, he could not break his promise. Just as Yuguro had said, no one in his own clan had questioned his story, and he was sure the Herders would accept it too.

But as they listened, their expressions changed and they fell silent. It was obvious they did not believe a word he said. Finally Toto the Elder removed the *nyokki* stick from his mouth and rested it on his knee. "Now listen here, Kassa boy," he said. "You just keep that lie shut up behind those lips of yours. We're not saying you have to tell us the truth if you don't want to, but we don't want to listen to lies."

Kassa's cheeks burned red. "What makes you think I'm lying?"

The Herder People looked at each other uncomfortably. Yoyo shrugged. "Kassa, you just don't smell like *lyokuhaku*."

"I don't smell like *lyokuhaku*? You mean stones smell?"

The Herders grinned. "Maybe not to you big people," Yoyo said, "but to us, all the stones in the caves have very strong scents."

Kassa frowned. "Are you making fun of me? Even if *lyokuhaku* does smell, of course I wouldn't smell like it. I gave it to Yuguro."

Toto scratched his chest noisily. "The smell of the stones in the cave doesn't fade away after just a day. Kassa boy, you've got a piece of *hakuma* on you now, right?"

Kassa started. It was true. He still carried the piece of *hakuma* he had found the other night inside his tunic.

Toto's sleepy-looking eyes suddenly widened and stared straight at him. "And that's not all. You smell like *luisha*, the luminous blue stone. I smelled it as soon as you stepped into this glade."

Kassa stared back at him, deeply shaken. The Herder People with whom he had lived since birth suddenly seemed like strangers.

Toto thumped his eagle chaser on the ground and stood up. "Hey there!" he said to his fellow Herders. "How long do you plan to rest? The Great Sun in the heavens will set before you know it!"

The tension in the air dissipated instantly as the others jumped to their feet. Thanking Kassa for the food, they hurried off to their work. Soon Kassa stood alone in Spring Hollow with Toto, who was in charge of the fire. He felt overcome with a desolate loneliness.

"Kassa boy." The Elder came over and grasped him by the elbow. Bent with age, he only reached Kassa's waist. "Thank you for the *losso*. You've a kind heart, lad." His grip tightened and he looked at Kassa intently. "No matter what they tell you, never trust anyone who would make a good boy like you lie. Remember: If there ever comes a time when you can't trust your own clan, think of us. We'll stand by you."

He let go and Kassa left the clearing without another word, his confusion shot through with a welcome bolt of

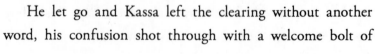

anger. *Well, of all the . . . What do the Herder People know anyway? How could there ever be a day when I can't trust my own people?*

He stepped out onto a rock ledge and the cold wind struck him full in the face. He clenched his teeth. But why had Yuguro trembled and turned so pale? Why had Kaguro looked as if he had seen a ghost? And who on earth was that woman?

No one was about to tell him the answers. The chieftain and Yuguro were hiding something important from their own people, from the clan. As he thought about the situation, the scenery spread out beneath him seemed to lose its color and grow distant.

"Do you have any idea who she is?" Kaguro was sunk in his chair, while Yuguro stood by the window. Turning to look at his brother, the younger man leaned back against the window frame, making it hard for Kaguro to see his expression against the westerly sun.

"Yes . . . When I defeated Jiguro, there was a girl there. She watched him die."

Kaguro frowned. "This is the first I've heard of it! Who was she? Jiguro's lover?"

"Perhaps. But I think she was too young for that."

"And? What did you do?"

"Nothing. I told her Jiguro was my older brother, but he was also a thief and a traitor and I had come to avenge the terrible crime he committed. Then I left her there. That was all. . . . What else could I have done? Are you suggesting I should have killed an innocent girl just because she might someday cause trouble?"

Kaguro opened his mouth but then shook his head wordlessly. He looked down and pressed his hand against his forehead. "Then there's no mistake," he continued after a pause. "She must be the traveler Kassa met." He looked up at Yuguro. "Could she be doing penance for Jiguro? But why would she come here now, after ten years have passed?"

Yuguro gazed out the window, his eyes narrowed. Finally he turned slowly back toward the room and walked over to the fireplace. "Perhaps she needed money."

Kaguro's brow furrowed. "You certainly come up with some wild ideas. What do you mean?"

"It's not a wild idea. Think about it. She defeated the *hyohlu* with her spear, which means that Jiguro must have taught her how to fight. What if he taught her more than that? If she needed money, wouldn't it be natural for her to think of the stones? Maybe she wasn't after *luisha*, but she could have sought *lyokuhaku*. And if Jiguro taught her how to find her way through the caves, then she could get it."

Comprehension dawned on Kaguro's face. "I see. You're right, that could be it. From what Kassa told us, she was using the marks on Jiguro's spear to find her way from New Yogo into Musa territory."

"Yes. And while she was passing through the caves, she

accidentally bumped into Kassa and Gina. She pretended to be a traveler doing penance and swore them to secrecy. It all fits together."

Kaguro sighed and shook his head. The old wound buried deep in his heart ached. "That good-for-nothing brother of ours. Wasn't it enough to bring shame upon our entire clan? Fifteen years of hell we suffered! But no, he had to go and leave *this* behind to cause trouble for us now!" He spat out the words and then rubbed the stub of his right arm. "If only I had still had my arm, I could have saved you so much pain. . . ."

He closed his eyes, and thus missed the slight smile that crossed Yuguro's lips.

"That's all in the past, brother. I merely vindicated the clan's honor. Leave the woman to me. I'll deal with her."

Kaguro raised his face. "What will you do?"

"It's a serious crime to steal *lyokuhaku*. I'll investigate quietly, and if she's done what I suspect, I'll have her executed — being careful, of course, not to let anyone else know her connection to Jiguro."

Kaguro grimaced. "I guess you're right. It's the only way."

"Yes," Yuguro murmured as he gazed at the flames, "It's the only way."

The chieftain's hall bustled with preparations for the feast celebrating the return of Yuguro and the chieftain's son, Kahm. Sweets and wine were distributed to the entire village, and the carousing continued far into the night.

Partway through the festivities, Yuguro signaled to his nephew Kahm and his brother-in-law Dom, who served as chief of the village guard. The three men quietly left the feast. Guiding the other two into the living room, Yuguro closed the heavy door, and the noise receded like a wave pulling back from the shore. He gestured for them to sit on the chairs. "I'm sorry to call you away from the feast. But we have a little problem on our hands."

Kahm and Dom looked at him with concern. "What kind of problem, uncle?" Kahm asked.

Yuguro smiled bleakly. "Well, it appears that a woman bearing Jiguro's spear has infiltrated the caves in our territory."

Shock showed on their faces, as if a ghost long dead had risen from the depths of darkness. "But how?" Dom muttered in a deep voice. He was a burly, broad-shouldered man, a head taller than even Yuguro. Although he was much more intelligent than his appearance suggested, he was also short-tempered.

Yuguro briefly recounted Kassa and Gina's tale and then explained what he had told Kaguro. When he finished, Dom grasped his shoulder.

"I understand, brother. I'll send five of our best guards after her. She'll stick out like a black goat among a white herd. We'll catch her in no time."

Yuguro shook his head. "You're right that we can find her easily. But I want you and Kahm to go after her yourselves."

He leaned forward and said quietly, "I trust you more than anyone else. You're the only ones I can count on."

Kahm and Dom flushed with pride.

Yuguro lowered his voice even further. "There are two reasons why we need to be cautious. First, we don't want this incident to bring back the memory of our clan's shame. Especially not now, at this crucial point in time." The two men nodded solemnly. "The second reason is a trifling thing, but still . . . The woman has a personal grudge against me." His lips twisted in a wry smile. "It's only to be expected, really. When I killed Jiguro, she screamed at me, vowing to avenge his death by destroying my honor. I didn't pay her any attention at the time — it was just the ranting of a girl."

He fixed his gleaming eyes on them. "I am sure you understand that at this important juncture, it will not do to have any doubt cast upon my honor, regardless of how ridiculous her claims may be."

Again, Kahm and Dom nodded gravely.

"When you capture her, there is no need to bring her back here for judgment. Jiguro apparently taught her to use a spear. Use that against her. Make her angry enough that she'll pick a fight. Then kill her. Kill her before she has a chance to ruin everything we've planned."

CHAPTER II
THE CAPTORS

Balsa and her aunt talked late into the night. Although tired, they were too agitated to sleep.

"You know, when I think about it, Kanbal has changed a lot in the last twenty years," Yuka said, her chin resting in her hand. "Each clan used to rule over its own territory, and even the king had no say in clan affairs. But since the time of King Rogsam, the king's power has grown stronger, so now almost all the young men from the chieftain's line go to live in the capital once they turn eighteen. They've formed a group known as the King's Circle, with the king and Yuguro at its head."

Balsa shrugged. She knew that each clan was like a little kingdom and marriage was only permitted within a clan. Having traveled through many lands, she found this exclusiveness oppressive. "Won't the country be stronger if the clans are united rather than separated?"

Her aunt frowned. "Yes, but only if it's an equal union with strong bonds among all the clans. Instead, the authority of the king and Yuguro Musa seem to be growing steadily greater than that of anyone else. . . . There's something suspicious about the whole setup."

As she listened to the wind shake the shutters, Balsa tried to remember the man named Yuguro. It had been autumn then, as it was now. He had arrived alone one day at the small hut in the Misty Blue Mountains where she and Jiguro lived with Tanda and his teacher, the magic weaver, Torogai. Jiguro's stunned reaction when he saw Yuguro was so unusual that Balsa feared he had resolved to let the man kill him.

But they had not fought — not immediately. The eight men who had found them before had taken a vow of silence, believing that Yoram would grant them his strength if they renounced speech with their opponent. Even if they had not taken this vow, in Kanbal, those who sought to avenge a crime were forbidden to converse with the criminal, for if they did, they would be defiled by the other's sin. No matter what Jiguro said, no matter how he pleaded, the eight had ignored him, attacking wordlessly.

But the man who called himself Yuguro was very talkative. On the night he arrived, he cheerfully introduced himself to Balsa as Jiguro's younger brother. He told them that

Rogsam was fatally ill, with only a few months to live, and spoke at length about their homeland. The two brothers talked for hours, finally lowering their voices to discuss something privately. Every night after that they went off into the forest, returning around dawn and sleeping until noon. Thinking that they must share some secret as brothers, Balsa never asked Jiguro what they were doing. But she was curious, and one night she could not help following them.

They trudged without torches to a dry, stony riverbed an hour's distance from Jiguro's hut. Despite the poor footing on the gravel, they took up battle stances, their spear tips gleaming white in the faint light of the crescent moon. Then they fought with wordless intensity — lunging, blocking, twisting, swinging — their movements so graceful it looked like they were dancing. The fight continued until the first rays of the sun broke over the dry river; then, without a word, they turned for home.

After almost a month, Yuguro left them. When he had gone, Jiguro said abruptly, "My older brother apparently lost his arm to a wolf bite. The Musa clan techniques passed down through the chieftain's line would have been lost. But this strange stroke of fortune has let me pass them on to my younger brother. At least that burden has been lifted from my shoulders."

Did Jiguro's brother betray him? Balsa wondered now. She remembered that that was when the gold ring had disappeared from Jiguro's spear. She had not asked him about it, simply assuming that he had given it to his brother as proof that he had passed on his skills, but now she realized that it might have had a much greater significance. Yuguro claimed to have defeated his older brother when he had not, and also to have retrieved the golden spear rings Jiguro had never stolen. And for his lies, he became a hero. "If Yuguro had the other eight gold rings, perhaps he stole them in the first place."

Aunt Yuka shook her head. "No. He couldn't have. When Jiguro left Kanbal, Yuguro was only sixteen. He still lived in Musa territory, not in the capital. It would have been impossible."

"Are you sure that he was only sixteen? He must have been much younger than Jiguro."

"Yes, I'm certain." Yuka sighed. "The land you grew up in is probably much more prosperous than Kanbal. Here a woman may have ten children and be lucky if four survive. It's not strange for children to be that far apart in age.

"Kaguro, Jiguro's older brother, should have been the first person sent to hunt him down. But he had been badly mauled by a wolf, and his arm was amputated. Yuguro would have been the logical choice after him, but at sixteen he was no match for Jiguro. In the end, Taguru was sent from our clan."

"Then only one person could have given the gold rings to Yuguro."

Yuka nodded, her face grim. "Yes. King Rogsam."

Balsa stared rigidly at her clenched fist. "What a clever way to bury Jiguro forever. And to make Yuguro his ally . . ."

"Well, I suppose we can guess all we want. But we don't have enough facts to judge what really happened." She stood up. "It's been hours since the midnight horn blew. We should go to bed soon."

Balsa nodded and stood up as well, but then she suddenly looked at her aunt. "Do you have rooms for patients to sleep here?" she asked.

Her aunt looked puzzled. "Yes, but why? We already prepared your bed in the guest room, remember?"

Balsa picked up her spear. "If there's a bed free in the house of healing, let me sleep there. You can tell people I'm the daughter of an old acquaintance and I need treatment for a chronic ailment. I may be overcautious, but I'd rather not get you into any trouble. You should tell the gardener I met this morning to keep quiet too."

"What are you saying?"

Balsa smiled at her. "It's nothing. I've just found that it's always safer to assume the worst. I don't want the goddess of fate sticking her tongue out at me."

Yuka complied without further protest. The moment Balsa had picked up her spear, she radiated the deadly aura of a warrior, and this, more forcefully than any words, had impressed upon Yuka the life her niece had been forced to lead.

Balsa stayed with her aunt for four days. Yuka was just as Jiguro had described her: an intelligent woman with more pluck than most men. She gave Balsa a room by herself, telling the other patients that she had to be isolated in case her condition was contagious, but Balsa spent most of her waking hours at her aunt's house.

The gardener was very loyal to Yuka, and it was clear that he would tell no one who Balsa was. Looking at the two of them, however, he scratched his neck and said in an undertone, "I'm surprised you haven't noticed it, Mistress Yuka, but she looks just like you. I wouldn't go out together in public if I were you."

His words surprised them. Neither one was the type to spend much time in front of a mirror, so they had not realized the resemblance until he mentioned it. Balsa thanked him and promised to stay out of sight. But it warmed her heart to think that there was someone living in this world whom she resembled.

Over those four peaceful days, Yuka spoke often of Balsa's parents and Jiguro, while Balsa shared stories of her life in New Yogo. Every day, they talked late into the night, chasing after the past, remembering those who had left this world. For Balsa, the time was like a dream that brought great joy.

But it did not last long. Just before noon on the fifth day, Balsa heard the sound of hooves on the wind. She paused in midstride as she was bringing goat's cheese up from her aunt's storage cellar. It sounded like a large company of men was approaching on horseback.

She looked out the window and saw ten riders cantering down from the village. Seven wore the badge of the Yonsa clan — the left ear of the thunder god — on the left side of their chests. Two others wore the badge of the Musa clan — the god's right ear — on the right side. And with them rode a man who was clearly a merchant, not a warrior.

Of course, Balsa thought. *The clothes merchant from Sula Lassal.*

"Balsa!" Her aunt came running up. "The guards are here. Hurry! The back door!"

Balsa shook her head. "It's impossible to escape them now. We're at the bottom of the valley. They'd see me at once. And besides, I don't know what story they've made up about me, but whatever it is, if I run away, it will seem like I've done something wrong."

Her aunt frowned. "But if you get caught . . . who knows what they might do to you?"

"The fact that they've come means that Yuguro guessed who I am, and thinks I'm in his way. Aunt Yuka, I want to know what he's planning. I want to know what was behind all this. I'm going to follow wherever this leads me. If I can't manage to find a way out in the end, I'll just have to accept it." She put her hand on her aunt's shoulder. "These last four days were wonderful. Thank you. From here on, we must become strangers again."

"What are you talking about?" her aunt retorted hotly. "If you think I'm going to stand by and see my only niece —"

Balsa gently squeezed her shoulder. "By myself, I can handle this. Please don't make me worry about you too." Yuka looked at her in surprise. Balsa gazed back steadily. "It will be better for me if we are strangers. Please understand."

Yuka hesitated a moment, then slowly nodded.

Outside, the guards dismounted from their horses. Spears in hand, they split into two groups to block the front and back entrances. Four men passed through the main gate: an imposing, heavily bearded guard from the Yonsa clan, the tall leathery merchant, and the two Musa warriors, one a towering giant and the other a young man wearing the green head scarf of the chieftain's line.

Yuka opened the door, her face hard and stern. "Captain Soosa, what on earth do you mean by making such a commotion?"

The bearded Yonsa warrior put his fist to his chest and bowed respectfully. "Mistress Yuka, I apologize for disturbing you. This is Captain Dom, leader of the Musa clan guard, and this is Master Kahm, eldest son of Chief Kaguro. They're pursuing a criminal who has fled into Yonsa territory and appears to have taken refuge in your house of healing."

Aunt Yuka looked at him sharply. "Criminal? And just what crime is this person accused of?"

"They're after a woman who entered the caves in Musa territory to steal *lyokuhaku.* She's hiding here."

"That's ridiculous! There's no such woman here."

The huge warrior named Dom took a step forward and looked down at her. "She has probably deceived you. We'll take a look around. If she's not here, then there's no harm done. But if she is, she could be dangerous and harm the patients if she's not handled properly. So please, stay calm and cooperate."

"Mistress Yuka, please," the captain said. "For the honor of our clan, we must cooperate with the Musa."

Yuka looked the three men squarely in the face. The younger man, Kahm, looked tense, but Dom and Soosa showed no sign of relenting as they returned her gaze. The merchant's eyes kept darting from her to the other men.

"I understand," she said finally. "You may do as you wish. But please go quietly. Some of my patients are very ill."

They moved quickly and carefully in their search of the building, but to Yuka it seemed forever before they arrived at Balsa's room. There was nothing she could do. She must leave it in her niece's hands.

"What about this room?"

"The daughter of an old friend is staying here. She suffers from terrible headaches, and her mother told her to come to me."

Yuka wondered if Balsa would leap out, spear in hand, to attack the men. But when the thick wooden door opened, the room was quiet. Balsa sat up slowly on the bed, as if she had only just been roused. The expression on her face gave no hint whatsoever that she was waiting to be captured. Yuka was astonished by her calm.

"What is it?" Balsa looked at them with a puzzled frown. The warriors entered the room, blocking the window and the door, and then glanced at the merchant. His eyes met Balsa's and he froze.

"Th — that's her. She's the one."

Before he had even finished, the men had drawn their daggers. The giant Dom thundered, "Woman! You have committed a terrible crime! We know for a fact that you unlawfully entered the caves in Musa territory to steal precious gems. Come quietly."

Balsa continued to stare at them in confusion. "What did you say? I'm not sure I understand. . . . It's true that I know this man. He's the clothes merchant from Sula Lassal, right? But how does that prove me a criminal?"

Dom laughed. "Nice try, woman. But we have two children who testified that they saw you deep in the caves."

Balsa gave a mental sigh. *Well, they certainly didn't lose any time before talking.*

"Yes, I entered the caves," she said out loud. "But I wasn't looking for jewels. I had a good reason to come from New Yogo to Musa territory. All I did was pass through the tunnels."

As he listened to her calm responses, a puzzled frown

creased Soosa's brow and he glanced uncertainly at the two men from the Musa clan. Dom and Kahm ignored him and continued to glare at Balsa.

She stood up slowly, keeping both hands in plain view. Then she cast a sharp look at Dom and Kahm. "I see," she said boldly, testing them. "So that's the kind of man who sent you. Rather than suggesting we talk it over, he plays a trick like this. . . . But I don't suppose you want me to explain why I came in front of someone from the Yonsa clan. Let me speak with your chief instead."

Dom and Kahm flushed. "If you're willing to come peacefully and be judged before the chief, then come," Kahm said quietly. "If you have something you wish to say, then you can say it at your trial. But be warned: My father is a stern man. He won't be fooled by your excuses."

Balsa let them bind her hands behind her back and lead her from the room. Dom grasped the rope and led her away while Kahm retrieved her spear and bag from under the bed. The captain of the Yonsa guard looked dissatisfied, but he also seemed relieved that Balsa had been taken without a fight.

Patients lined both sides of the hallway, staring at Balsa with frightened faces as she walked past. She bowed slightly to Yuka, who was waiting at the front door. "Mistress Yuka, I'm sorry to have caused you trouble. These men are mistaken. I'll return when I've cleared my name and pay for my treatment then."

Yuka looked into her eyes, wondering what words of encouragement she could offer, only to be startled by what she saw there. Although her hands were bound and she was held captive, Balsa's eyes were filled with a fierce light, like a fighter ready to enter the ring.

CHAPTER III
THE POISONED SPEAR TIP

The cloaks of Balsa's captors flapped noisily in the wind. Dom and Kahm placed her astride a small horse and mounted horses on either side of her. Each held one end of the rope that bound her. Balsa did not look around, although she could feel her aunt's gaze boring into her back. Narrowing her eyes against the glare and the sand whipped up by the wind, she considered her situation. From Dom and Kahm's reaction to her challenge, it was clear that Yuguro had told them something about her, and that they had concealed whatever it was from the Yonsa guards, convincing them that she was a thief who had broken clan law.

No one spoke during the hour-long journey to the border between the two territories. When they reached the forts at the border post, Captain Soosa looked about uneasily. "There are no reinforcements to meet you. Would you like me to lend you two of my riders?"

Dom laughed and waved off the offer. "No, no. Thanks, but we wouldn't want people to think Musa warriors need more than two men to escort a mere woman! Really, there's no need to bother."

"Captain Soosa," Kahm added, "your assistance was very helpful. We won't forget what you did for us."

The captain looked somewhat mollified by his sincerity. "Don't mention it. Farewell, then."

When the Yonsa guards had ridden away, Dom beckoned to the merchant, who was hanging back. Avoiding Balsa's eyes, the man brought his mount closer, and Dom dropped several jingling silver coins into his hand. "Thanks for your help catching this criminal. You can follow the valley road from here to Sula Lassal. We're going back by the mountain road."

The merchant looked at him beseechingly and whispered, "You don't think she'll come looking for me, do you?"

Dom grinned. "No. I guarantee it."

The merchant bowed his head, kicked his horse into a gallop, and sped away as fast as he could.

"So, shall we be off?" Dom thumped Balsa roughly on the back with his huge hand. If the movement of his arm had not warned her, she would have tumbled off her horse. As it was, she barely managed to cushion the blow by leaning forward just before he struck, and the force of it still knocked the breath out of her. "Good reflexes, I see," Dom sneered. "Jiguro must have beaten you often."

His words hurt far more than the actual blow, but she remained expressionless. She knew instinctively that she must not show any anger.

Behind her, Kahm gritted his teeth. Even though they were following his uncle's orders, it seemed unfair to goad their prisoner into fighting just so they could kill her. Dom, however, seemed to be enjoying it. As they rode along the mountain path, through the shade of scattered clumps of trees, he kept up his criticism of Jiguro. He also kept bumping into Balsa's horse, which was already struggling to navigate the stony track. If he succeeded in unhorsing her, she would be badly injured or, worse, killed when she smashed her head on the rocks.

By now, Balsa was sure that was exactly what Dom wanted.

As the sun began to sink in the sky and the shadows of the shrubs lengthened, they came to a clear stream surrounded by grass and a grove of trees. Balsa was drenched in sweat and gasping from the effort of keeping her seat. Her throat burned from the strong, dry wind.

"Master Kahm, let's rest here a little. Our prisoner seems a bit tired," Dom said, dismounting. He pulled Balsa from her horse and tied her to a tree, but bound the rope carelessly, so she could feel how loose it was. Kahm brought over her spear, and Dom placed it beside her at the foot of the tree. Then the two men went over to the stream, washed their faces, and drank thirstily. When he had finished, Kahm dipped a water skin into the stream. Dom looked at him suspiciously.

"We're only thirty *lon* away from the village. What do you need water for?"

"I thought I'd give her a drink," Kahm answered.

Dom snatched the skin from his hands and threw it on the ground. "What do you think you're doing? That's no woman over there. She's nothing but trash come to destroy our dream!"

The blood rose hotly in Kahm's face. "She's not trash! Even if we have to kill her, I can't stand to do it like this. It's so dirty, underhanded . . ."

Balsa brought her ragged breathing under control, listening carefully to the two men. She no longer felt dizzy and her vision had cleared. She slipped the rope off her hands and rubbed them. Wiping the sweat from her brow, she watched the men argue. Kahm's profile suddenly reminded her of Jiguro, and she remembered with shock that the young man was his nephew. It seemed ironic that she should end up fighting Jiguro's own kin, but she certainly couldn't stand by and let them kill her.

Let's get on with it, then, she thought. She rolled her neck once and then clapped her hands loudly to attract their attention. They started and glanced around as she stood up, laughing. "You certainly like to complicate things. So basically you're just looking for a good excuse to kill me, right? Like me attacking you. So what if I just stand here and do nothing — if I don't fight or run? What will you do then?"

Dom slapped his spear against the palm of his hand. "Well, I suppose the result would be the same now, wouldn't it? All we'd have to do was *say* that you had attacked us. . . . There're no other witnesses, are there? Believe me, I would've got this over with a lot sooner if I didn't have to consider the feelings of the chieftain's son here."

Kahm looked at him in surprise. "You had to consider *my* feelings?"

"Yes. Master Yuguro knows you very well, you see. I know you can't help it because you're still young, but if you'll forgive my lecturing you, Master Kahm, when you have an important job to do, you shouldn't worry about bloodying your hands."

Kahm ground his teeth. "I'm not worried about getting my hands dirty!" he spat. "I'm saying that if we have to kill her, then we should give her back her spear and kill her in a fair fight. We should let her die with honor."

Balsa ran her hand through her hair. "Master Kahm," she said. "You appear to be a much better man than that hulk over there, but I'm afraid you're still wrong." She looked at him steadily. "Whether it's a fair fight or not, honor makes no difference to the one who dies. Honor is nothing but an empty word to comfort the killer. Your uncle Jiguro knew that well."

She looked up at Dom. "So, Master Giant, I took your taunts in the hope of meeting Yuguro, but I see no reason to put up with this any longer if you intend to kill me anyway."

Dom's mouth twisted into a scornful smile. "Oh? You intend to fight? How kind of you. Master Kahm, you must rejoice. It seems you'll get your chance for what you call a 'fair fight.'"

Balsa laughed. "Who said anything about fighting?" She swept up her spear and disappeared into the forest.

Dom's face turned red with rage. "You!" He raced after her, but just when he reached the grove, something whipped through the air and smacked him in the eye. He jumped back with a cry. The end of the rope that had bound Balsa had hit him.

Kahm saw Balsa leap out from the trees. Dom reacted instantly, swinging his spear toward her, but Balsa was faster by far. Blocking his spear with her own, she swept it aside in a wide arc, then punched the butt end of her spear straight into his nose. It broke audibly, and Dom pitched over backward.

But strength was his pride and, as he fell, he whipped his spear out sideways. Balsa leapt over it and drove the point of her own spear deep into his shoulder with all her weight behind it. He screamed. Without batting an eyelash, she stepped on his arm and yanked out her spear.

Kahm watched numbly. He had never seen Dom beaten so soundly before. In fact, he had never seen a real spear fight, so he failed to notice that Balsa refrained from striking the final blow.

She moved away from Dom where he writhed in agony on the ground and turned toward Kahm. "So how about it? Do you want to fight too?"

His knees were shaking, but he clenched his teeth and leveled his spear at her. She nodded and moved easily to close the space between them. He focused, drawing energy from deep within to fight.

At that moment, however, Dom threw his spear, aiming straight for Balsa's back.

Even she had not foreseen this move. He was still prostrate on the ground, and was forced to throw it left-handed. Moreover, if she moved aside, it would strike Kahm. By the time she sensed the danger, she barely had time to twist away. The spear point grazed her shoulder, giving Kahm just enough time to knock it to the ground.

"You're finished," Dom jeered. "I coated the tip with *togal.*"

Balsa felt the wound in her shoulder grow numb and knew he spoke the truth; the spear had been poisoned. She had run out of time. Turning around, she raced toward Kahm, knocked aside the spear he swung toward her, and hit him in the pit of the stomach with the hilt of her own. He crumpled to the ground in a dead faint. Without pausing to look back, Balsa splashed through the creek and into the trees, heading up the mountain.

The sun had already set, but the sky still glowed with a lingering blue light. The numbness spread from the wound in her left shoulder to her back and chest. She let it bleed, praying that some of the poison would wash out with it, and continued to climb.

Finally the last light faded and everything sank into darkness. Nothing moved except the occasional mountain goat bounding away from her in fright, its hooves ringing on the stones. The numbness spread to her legs, and suddenly they slipped out from under her. She fell between two rocks, hitting her side as she went down. Balsa lost consciousness.

CHAPTER IV
THE ERMINE RIDERS

"How many times do I have to tell you? Never let down your guard! Never, never turn your back on an enemy, even if you think you've beaten him!"

Balsa opened her eyes with a start. *Jiguro?*

But she heard nothing more. A white blur hovered before her eyes, and she felt weights pressing against her chest and back. Gradually her mind cleared and she remembered where she was. She was lying on her side on a mountain in Musa territory, where she had fallen between the rocks. She still felt numb, but judging from the fact that she was alive, the poison had not been enough to kill her.

With relief, she found that she could move her right arm, which was pinned beneath her. She squirmed and wriggled, gasping for breath, until she managed to sit up. Leaning back against the rock, she pulled her legs toward her and breathed deeply.

The tops of the bumpy crags above her glowed white. *The moon must have risen,* she thought. But it was more than the moon; everything around her seemed unnaturally bright. Occasionally she heard the pitter-patter of a mouse or some other little creature running, and then the beating of owl wings in pursuit. Perhaps the poison in her veins had lent her this extraordinary perception.

Now what am I going to do? She gazed at the strange moonlit world. When she was captured, she had intended to let Dom and Kahm take her to Yuguro. But she realized now that Yuguro would never risk being stripped of his mask as a hero. He would never give her a chance to defend herself, but would kill her first, finding some excuse to justify his actions.

She knew from bitter experience that authority meant power. She might be skilled as a warrior, but she did not stand a chance against a man as influential as Yuguro. If one person could really make a difference, she, Jiguro, and her father would not have been forced to suffer. *I guess all I can do is escape with my life. . . .*

She thought of the years she and Jiguro had spent on the run. To thwart Rogsam by escaping his clutches, to survive, was the only way to show defiance. *What an insignificant life!* A deep sadness rose inside her. *Never to produce anything, never to create something, to live only to survive, like the rock mice that flee from the owl. . . .*

Just then she glimpsed a tiny flicker of light in the shadow of a boulder. *A firefly?* she wondered. But it was far too cold for fireflies, and they lived near water, not on the dry, craggy slopes. Suddenly it shot off, leaving a long trail of pale blue light in its wake. It bounced onto the top of one rock and then quickly flitted to another.

She recalled a story her mother had told her when she was very young. *Never go up the rocks when the moon is bright. That's when the Titi Lan, the Ermine Riders, go hunting. The Titi Lan are small but fierce. If you disrupt their hunt, they'll curse you and you'll lose your mind.*

It can't be, Balsa thought. Looking around, she noticed many other bright specks flitting here and there. She watched them intently, being careful not to give herself away. Ordinarily, it would have been too dark to see, but with the poison in her veins, the scene unfolded clearly, like something out of a dream.

A small ermine stood across from her on top of a rock. The light of the moon gleamed like frost on its smooth fur. On its back sat a tiny little man. In his right hand, he held a slender spear, and in his left, a long-handled light. The handle, she realized, was actually a stem with a flower dangling from the end. Something inside the blossom glowed with a soft blue light.

The ermine and its rider both lifted their faces and

sniffed the air. Balsa prayed that they would not detect her scent. She saw them tense suddenly and watched as a beetle, drawn perhaps by the light, flew toward them. The little man's spear pierced it faster than sight, but it was too big for him to handle. He struggled desperately to capture the flapping insect, which was almost half his size.

Balsa heard the beat of wings and glanced up. An owl was diving straight for the Titi Lan. Without pausing to think, she grabbed a small stone that lay beneath her hand and threw it at the owl. It missed, but the startled bird veered upward. Alerted by the flapping of its wings, the Titi Lan and his mount disappeared under the boulder in a flash.

Balsa heaved a sigh. Had that really happened, or was the poison making her hallucinate? By now, she was fairly sure she had a fever. Because she had sweated so much earlier, the chill of the night air pierced her all the more, and yet it would not do to light a fire. The cold was beginning to take its toll. She slid her back down the rock until she was lying on the ground.

She dozed off, then woke suddenly, sensing something in the darkness. Still, however, she felt no danger. Opening her eyes slowly, she saw in front of her a blue light . . . and a very small face.

A youth with white hair and red eyes was staring at her. He was so small, he could have fit inside her hand, but his face was perfectly proportioned. His clothes were made of grass fiber and insect wings. "Toh Lan, Big Hunter," he greeted her in Kanbalese, in a voice that sounded like an insect chirping. Balsa blinked gently to show that she was listening, afraid that he would vanish if she spoke.

"Thank you for saving my life. Now Titi Lan will repay you by saving your life." His eyes strayed to the cut on her shoulder and then back to her face. "That smells of *togal*, the poison that the Toh Kal, the Big Brothers, use to fight eagles. They have the antidote. I'll bring them to you."

Balsa shook her head slightly. In the quietest voice possible, she whispered, "I thank you for your kindness, but the Big Hunters are hunting me. Please don't bring them."

Titi Lan smiled. "I didn't say that I would bring the Big Hunters. I said I would bring the Big *Brothers*." He stepped back a few paces. Putting his fingers to his mouth, he whistled sharply. A similar whistle sounded from the shadows, followed by another, and then another farther away, as if a messenger was running ahead. Shortly after, she heard a whistle that was louder than those of the Titi Lan, and then several footsteps.

Through the haze of fever, she saw a face gazing at her. It belonged to an old man as small as a child. *The Herder People*, she thought. She remembered the young Herder boys with whom she used to play and climb the mountains as a child.

She heard the old man say quietly, "Titi Lan, Ermine Rider, we came when we heard your whistle. But who's this?"

"I don't know," the Titi Lan responded. "But she saved my life when I was attacked by an owl, so I wish to save hers. She has been poisoned with *togal*. She said she's being hunted."

Balsa felt a hand placed gently on her wound. "It smells of *togal* all right. And of iron. She must have been hit by a spear. . . . Chil Kal, Little Brother, we'll take care of her. Go back to your hunt while the moon is still bright."

"Many thanks, Toh Kal! Long may your goats thrive and leap on the mountains."

His voice was the last thing Balsa remembered as she faded from consciousness.

She was once again twenty-four years old, and Jiguro was dying. His face had grown thin and gaunt, wasted by illness. She found the sight of him hard to bear. It seemed so unfair that this man, who had sacrificed so much for her, should now be tormented by disease. His eyes were closed, and she whispered fervently in his ear, "I promise you, I'll atone for my father's sin. I'll save the lives of eight men to make up for what he did. Please, rest easy."

He opened his eyes a crack and looked at Balsa. "It's much harder to help people than to kill them," he said. "Don't be so hard on yourself, Balsa." A smile touched his lips. "I'll sink beneath the Yusa mountains, the mother range, and atone for my sins myself." Grasping his hand, she closed her eyes and clenched her teeth. Jiguro returned her grip.

"Balsa, I've been thinking while I was lying here dreaming. I've been asking myself whether I would have made a different choice at any point in my life." She looked at him quickly and saw that his eyes were smiling. "And I came to the conclusion that I'd still choose the same path, even if I were given the chance to return to my youth and start all over again. I've always chosen the only road possible. So I have no regrets."

He clasped her hand more tightly still. "My one concern is that I couldn't set you free. I couldn't erase my own shadow from your heart."

Balsa put her other hand over his, wrapping it in both her hands. "That I will do myself."

Jiguro's smile deepened. "You've always had an anger that burned deep inside you. It's helped you, yet it's also been a curse. If you can just get through to the other side of that anger, you'll be more at peace."

Balsa dreamed again — this time that someone lifted her up and carried her underground. She heard many voices whispering and tasted bitter water. She swallowed, and as the liquid seeped through her, her body gradually relaxed.

Far into the night, when all was silent and cold, Balsa regained consciousness briefly. Between the rocks, she glimpsed the sky, pale blue with the dawn. As she gazed at it, she felt her mind grow clear and empty. *Maybe it's time to break through my anger.* Instead of running from the owl's talons, she would run up them, and sink her teeth into the owl's neck. Only then would it understand the rock rat's pain.

I have no noble reason. I just want to get even. That's all. She smiled bitterly. She could see this now so clearly. . . . She would follow this meaningless but undeniable feeling to the very end and see what was on the other side.

She fell into a deep and dreamless sleep.

CHAPTER I
THE KING'S ENVOYS

Rumors spread rapidly through the clan settlement that the chieftain's son and the captain of the guard had returned badly wounded. The frightened clothes merchant terrified all the shopkeepers in the marketplace with his story of the fierce woman who defeated the two men. To prevent the tale from being embellished any further, Chief Kaguro called a gathering of the warriors.

As Kassa was of spear-bearing age, he was permitted to sit in the farthest corner of the great hall. Surrounded by the noise of the crowd, he looked for his cousin Kahm, but was startled when he finally caught sight of him. Although Kahm's injury had been slight — just a few cracked ribs, now firmly supported by a wide leather belt — his face appeared haggard and his expression grim. To Kassa, he looked like a different person. Kaguro thumped the stone floor sharply

with the butt of his spear and the crowd fell silent. His deep voice resonated throughout the room. "Clansmen. I have called you here today because, as I'm sure you've heard, an incident has occurred that seriously threatens the honor of our clan. Yuguro will tell you the details."

Yuguro took a step forward. A shaft of sunlight shone through a narrow window and illuminated his figure. "My clansmen, a ghost has come back to haunt us. The ghost of one whom those over thirty will remember well, a man that I myself laid to rest with these two hands." A low murmur ran through the hall. Kassa saw his father's face tighten. "That's right. The man that both the chieftain and I have been ashamed to call our brother, the wickedest man in Kanbal — Jiguro."

He gave a small sigh. "I was only sixteen when Jiguro fled this country, stealing the gold rings that symbolize the bond between the royal family and the clans. My father had died of illness and my esteemed older brother had lost his right arm. If our family had not suffered these misfortunes, or if I had been a young man in my twenties, then the strongest youth of the other eight clans would not have died.

"Jiguro was very strong. I know this well, for I was the last to fight him. But his heart was rotten to the core. And so I didn't hesitate to kill him, even though he was my own brother."

A hush had fallen over the hall. Recalling those days when they had lived in shame, the older men remembered with renewed pride the triumphant young Yuguro returning as a hero. The younger men knew this story too, but it was their first time to hear it from his own mouth, and they listened with rapt attention.

"I never told anyone this before, but when I fought Jiguro, someone was watching us — a young woman of about twenty-two or twenty-three. I defeated Jiguro fairly and gave him the honor of dying in battle, but the young woman cursed me."

Kahm felt a sharp pain in his side and rubbed a hand over his broken ribs. The words the woman had said as she swept back her sweat-drenched hair popped into his mind. *Whether it's a fair fight or not, honor makes no difference to the one who dies. Honor is nothing but an empty word to comfort the killer. Your uncle Jiguro knew that well.*

"I merely did what was right. But women . . ." Yuguro smiled. "You can never tell what they're thinking, if you know what I mean."

The crowd laughed, but Kahm did not smile. The spear-woman he had faced was far removed from the picture his uncle was now painting.

"As I was saying, she cursed me. She vowed to make a fool of me and shame my honor. I paid no attention to these threats and completely forgot about her. But now we've found out that she has come to Kanbal. Tonno! Kassa!"

Kassa jumped when Yuguro suddenly called him forward. His father hastily beckoned him and together they went to stand by Yuguro's side. Kassa was so nervous, he could not even remember how he made it to the front. He could see only row upon row of curious faces wondering what this was all about.

Yuguro placed a large, heavy hand on his shoulder. "I'm sure you all know Kassa's younger sister, Gina, my niece. She's a lot like my sister, a very brave girl."

Laughter erupted from a group of Kassa's friends.

"Apparently, Gina wished to show my son a thing or two, and she went into the caves to prove her courage. Her older brother, Kassa, went after her to save her. And there they met the woman I've been telling you about as she was making her way through the caves from New Yogo."

Kassa was surprised. What Yuguro had said was true, but he had failed to mention the fact that they were attacked by the *hyohlu* and the woman had saved them. He had missed the most important part of the story. . . . Kassa opened his mouth to speak, but Yuguro's hand tightened on his shoulder. He looked beseechingly at his father. Tonno just shook his head faintly.

"She told Kassa and Gina that she was on a journey of penance and asked them not to tell anyone. Now Kassa may be young, but he's a true Musa warrior. He saw danger in the fact that a stranger could be in the caves, and he came and told me immediately. I rewarded him and Tonno for providing such precious information. To prevent rumors from spreading, I told them to say they'd found a piece of *lyokuhaku*."

Kassa was speechless with shock. He felt as though he were in a bad dream. Was this some carefully thought-out strategy that only adults could understand? Yuguro had spun his words cleverly, weaving the facts together to make a completely different story. Yet Kassa could not bring himself to correct him. The eyes of the crowd intimidated him, and if Yuguro did have some deeper plan, he might ruin it by speaking up.

"I'm very impressed with Kassa here. He may be small, but he's brave and clever." Yuguro smiled at him. Hesitantly, Kassa smiled back. When Yuguro gestured for him to return to his seat, he walked shakily through the crowd to the back. Men patted him on the shoulder, saying, "Well done," but he could not respond.

"So once I discovered this woman had infiltrated Kanbal, I immediately sent Kahm and Dom after her. They did a superb job, quickly finding and capturing her where she was hiding in Yonsa territory. That was yesterday."

Yuguro gestured for Kahm to come to his side. "As you all know, Kahm and Dom are both excellent spearmen. Well, Kahm is still a little young, but nevertheless, he's close to being one of the best. So I had complete confidence that they could capture her."

He sighed, looked at Kahm, and then looked back to the assembled men. "But this woman is as cunning as a wolf. When they arrived in the mountains, she fell off her horse on purpose and pretended to be wounded. Dom was dismounting to help her when she suddenly spooked the horses. He fell and broke his nose, while Kahm here cracked his ribs. Dom still tried to stop her, but she stabbed him in the shoulder with her spear. Then she fled into the mountains. Isn't that right, Kahm?"

Kahm looked up at his uncle, sick at heart. He revered Yuguro and knew that this deception was necessary if their great undertaking was to succeed. But piling one lie on top of another went against his honest nature, and he hated it.

Yuguro's eyes narrowed sharply. "I'm not blaming you for your failure, you know," he said gently. "You're young and you were hurt. There's no need to be ashamed of not helping Dom when he fought on with his broken nose, or for letting the woman escape."

Kahm looked at his uncle in shock. "No! That's not true! Dom was —"

His father, Kaguro, cut him off. "Kahm! You should be ashamed of yourself. Don't try to excuse your cowardice by blaming someone who isn't here!"

Kahm was stunned. Dom's injury was fairly serious, but certainly not awful enough to prevent him from attending this meeting. He had heard Yuguro himself tell him not to come, advising him to rest instead. Kahm ground his teeth. He felt an invisible net tightening around him, for anything he said now would sound like he was making excuses. His only choice was to remain silent.

"Kahm is still young, brother," Yuguro said calmly.

"Don't be too hard on him." He turned back to the crowd. "Well, it was a long story, but now you know the situation. Clearly this woman has escaped into Musa territory. As she fled without her cape or supplies, she won't survive long in this season. Still, I'd like fifty of our best men to divide up and search for her. Get the Herder People to help too." Then he added with a smile, "But don't underestimate her cunning or her skill with the spear, and don't be fooled by anything she says about me."

The men laughed.

At that moment, a horn blast echoed long and high, weaving through their laughter. The room fell silent, then the men began talking excitedly again. The horn signaled the arrival of a message from the king of Kanbal.

There came a loud knock, and the young men guarding the doors opened them. Two warriors stepped into the hall wearing the purple cloaks and silver headscarves that marked them as the king's envoys. The crowd hushed immediately. Facing Yuguro, one of the men held high a scroll of goat's hide sealed with wax.

"Greetings to Kaguro Musa, Chieftain of the Musa Clan, and Master Yuguro," he announced in clear, ringing tones. "We bear an urgent message from the king for Master Yuguro."

They walked forward under the eager gaze of the warriors, who were hoping desperately for news of the Giving Ceremony. After the messenger handed Yuguro the scroll, he bowed, broke the seal, and opened it. He read it without a word, then looked at the messengers.

"You have traveled far and fast to deliver this. I'll start preparing immediately. We'll be ready to leave the day after tomorrow. Please rest and refresh yourselves here until that time." He gestured to two of his attendants and they led the messengers from the hall. Then Yuguro turned to face the assembly.

"Clansmen, great news! The Gate to the Mountain Deep has opened."

The men gasped and then, as the news sank in, they raised a thunderous cheer.

Deep within a cave behind the king's castle lay a massive door of natural rock that barred the way into the Mountain Deep. It could only be opened from the inside, but once every generation, the Gate slid open, signaling that the Mountain King would hold the Giving Ceremony in the winter of that year, and bestow much-needed *luisha* upon the people of Kanbal. Although there had been occasional discrepancies in timing, previous ceremonies had always been about two decades apart. But this time twenty years had passed, and then thirty, with no sign of the Gate being opened, and the people of Kanbal had grown steadily poorer and more anxious. Some whispered that the sacred bond between Kanbal and the Mountain King had been violated since the last Dancer, Jiguro, had dared to steal the gold rings of the King's Spears and flee the country. . . .

Now, after thirty-five years, word had finally come. The ceremony would take place this winter. The bond between the two kingdoms had not been severed after all! The men's faces shone with joy. When their king received the *luisha*, grain would once again flow into the country. He would present every clan with gifts. For the next few years at least, they would not have to worry about having enough food for the winter. For the people of Kanbal, this announcement answered all their hopes and relieved all their fears.

"Everything seems to be happening at once!" Yuguro called over the tumult in the room. "Men, there's much to be done. Divide up the work. The gifts for the Mountain King must be ready by the day after tomorrow." The men began talking excitedly. Yuguro thumped his spear butt on the floor to regain their attention. "I've just had a thought for which I would ask your approval." He beckoned his eldest son, Shisheem, who was standing nearby. He was almost the same height as his father. "Ordinarily, Kahm would attend me in the capital, but as you can see, he is injured. A ten-day horse ride will be too taxing for him. Instead, I propose to take my son, Shisheem, who turned sixteen this year. It's time for him to mix with the other sons of the clan chieftains and learn from them. What do you say?"

Kahm turned pale and looked first at his uncle, then at his father. But Kaguro merely nodded to Yuguro, a bitter expression on his face. If he agreed, no one else would even think of opposing the idea.

"Don't worry, Kahm," Yuguro said to him. "The Gate to the Mountain Deep has opened, but it will be another twenty-five days or so before we actually enter the mountain for the ceremony. Follow me to the capital when you feel better." Then he turned to the clansmen and shouted, "Men of the Musa clan — it's time to work!"

Kassa was pushed along with the boisterous crowd as they left the hall, but he turned for one last look at Kahm. Just before he passed through the doors, he caught sight of him and Shisheem. The contrast between their two faces — one dark and gloomy, the other flushed and shining — remained branded on his mind.

CHAPTER II
JIGURO'S NEPHEWS

For two days after the king's envoys arrived, the village was caught up in a whirlwind of activity. The women rolled up bright wool tapestries and wrapped *laga* in clean cloth. The men decorated the carts that would carry these gifts until they were satisfied that they would outshine those of the other clans.

Then Yuguro, Shisheem, and thirty attendants rode off amid the cheers of their clansmen. Kahm and his father, their thoughts bitter, stood watching the glorious procession recede into the distance.

Kahm's injury was slight, but he had spent the last two days closeted in his room, reluctant to meet anyone. He found that being alone gave him the chance to think things through. He felt betrayed by his uncle, which hurt all the more because he had worshipped him since childhood. He had spent more of his life with Yuguro than with his own father.

A seed of doubt sprang up in his heart: *Would Uncle Yuguro make Shisheem his attendant for the Giving Ceremony?* He could be overreacting. Yet no matter how he looked at it, his uncle's version of the story seemed designed to disgrace Kahm and convince everyone that Shisheem should accompany him to the capital.

Traditionally, only those who had participated in the Giving Ceremony as attendants were chosen as the next King's Spears. If the attendants returned alive from the Mountain Deep, they were promoted to Spear when they reached the age of twenty. If one of the chosen died or became crippled before the next ceremony, the King's Spears gathered together to select a new candidate from his clan. A Spear who had participated as an attendant at the age of sixteen or seventeen would be in his mid-thirties by the time of the next ceremony — intellectually and physically in his prime. So it had been for centuries.

But then tragedy had struck, for all the young men chosen as attendants had been slain by Jiguro, and the interval between the ceremonies had lasted too long. They had been forced to change the system. Ten years earlier, the clans had held a tournament before the king to choose nine new Spears from the best warriors of the chieftains' lines. Yuguro, naturally, had been selected from the Musa clan.

If the ceremony had been held at the usual twenty-year

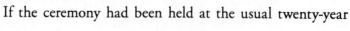

126

interval, Kahm would have been the right age. But now he was thirty-one, which was old for an attendant, and his eldest son, Kahmuro, who lived with his mother in the capital, had only just turned nine. Shisheem, on the other hand, was sixteen, the perfect age to serve. Kahm's jaw clenched. *Does Uncle Yuguro plan to make me stay in Musa as the next chieftain while Shisheem becomes a Spear?*

Ordinarily he would have accepted this fate with good grace despite his disappointment. But it was at this ceremony that Yuguro would launch the plan they had been developing for some time — a plan so secret not even Chief Kaguro knew about it. Kahm had worked so hard on this plan; he could not bear to be excluded now.

Another suspicion gnawed at his mind. He had not known that Dom's spear was smeared with poison. Such foul play was inconceivable. Had Dom been acting on his own initiative, or under someone else's orders? And why would he have thrown the spear, knowing it could hit Kahm? Had he been hoping to kill both him and the woman?

Kahm dismissed the thought. *That's impossible. I must be reading too much into it.* If he had died from *togal* poisoning, it would have exposed their plot to kill the woman without a fair trial. And surely his uncle would not try to murder him. . . .

Still, what an amazing spear-wielder! Never had he seen anyone move like that woman. Not even the Spears, the greatest warriors in Kanbal, could compare to her speed and agility. If Jiguro taught her, he must have been a true master.

Suddenly he recalled something his father had said long ago, when they had been watching Yuguro train the warriors in the yard in front of the hall. His father, who would never wield a spear again, had a bleak expression on his face that made Kahm sad. Yuguro moved with skill and finesse and seemed to thoroughly enjoy displaying his superior strength.

"Too much wasted movement," Kaguro had remarked abruptly.

Kahm did not respond. He thought that his father must speak from envy, although he could see no trace of jealousy in his profile. Rather, he seemed to be gazing at something in the distance.

"Jiguro was far better."

Kahm could hardly believe what he heard. Jiguro's name was taboo. None of the Musa clan ever mentioned him, and his father and uncle in particular never spoke of him. And yet his father continued, "I suppose it's hard for you to believe, but I was always a better spearman than Yuguro. But Jiguro . . ." Following his brother's movements with his one good eye, he muttered, "Jiguro was a genius. A warrior like that might appear once in a hundred years. That's why my father chose him rather than me for the Giving Ceremony, even though I was the eldest.

"And he fulfilled my father's expectations. He was chosen as the Dancer. No sixteen-year-old attendant had ever served as the Dancer before."

Kahm knew that all the King's Spears and their attendants competed in a tournament in the Mountain Deep to determine which one was the strongest. The victor became the Dancer and dueled one of the *hyohlu*, the Guardians of the Darkness and servants to the Mountain King. Only when the Dancer defeated the *hyohlu* did the Mountain King open the Last Door and invite the king of Kanbal, his Spears, and their attendants to enter his palace. Beyond that door, it was said, lay a vast castle made of *luisha*, the most beautiful gem in the world.

"But instead of bringing honor to our clan, his skill brought misfortune on the whole country." His father heaved a deep sigh as he stared over the practice field. "But you know, to be honest, even if I had been the one to go after him, I don't think I could have beaten him." He lowered his voice. "Which is why I think that Jiguro must have let Yuguro kill him."

At the time, Kahm had been disappointed in his father, believing that he belittled Yuguro's feat out of envy. But now, as he recalled those words, new questions began to run through his mind. *What kind of man could have trained a spearwoman like that? What did she really see when Yuguro fought Jiguro?* His heart began to pound. *And what if she saw something other than the glorious victory Yuguro proclaimed to the world? If she did, then I could see why he might use poison.*

He closed his eyes and forced himself to calm down. *That's impossible. . . . Damn! How can I think such things just because he was hard on me this once? He'd never do something like that. After all, he's the one who saved Kanbal by bringing back all nine spear rings.* He shook his head sharply. Using poison was not in his uncle's character, although he wouldn't put it past Dom. He decided that Dom must have been acting on his own.

Opening his eyes, he looked up at the thick, smoke-blackened beams exposed in the ceiling. Once a year, the king sent Yuguro to the kingdoms of New Yogo and Sangal to barter *luisha* for grain, and Kahm had often accompanied him. The residences of New Yogo ministers were built of smooth unvarnished wood, and the walls were often covered in gorgeous brocade tapestries. Even the merchants wore clothes of finely woven silk. And in Sangal, he had seen breathtaking mosaics of luminescent shells on the walls of ordinary government officials.

Yet even the halls of our chieftains are no better than this, Kahm thought as he gazed at the rough ceiling. True, commoners in those countries lived very frugal lives. He remembered the native Yakoo in Yogo in particular as extremely poor. But if they starved because of a bad harvest one year, they could look forward to a plentiful harvest the next.

In contrast, there was hardly any land worth farming in Kanbal. The north was covered by tall snowcapped mountain peaks, while the soil in the southern lowlands was so poor that nothing grew there besides the tall pines. Only the highland plateaus where the clan settlements were scattered could really be farmed. Yet even here, strong winds blew the soil away so that each year the land grew more barren. All the people could count on was milk and meat from the mountain goats that populated the rocky crags, and *gasha*, which grew despite the poor soil. And it was thanks to the plentiful springs, which gushed from beneath the mountain, that they could grow anything at all. Thus most Kanbalese men, even those who belonged to the warrior class, had to work in New Yogo or Sangal every winter. Some of them settled in Yogo and lived there the rest of their lives. Without *luisha* to buy grain, the poor mountain country of Kanbal could not have survived.

Kahm sighed deeply. *I guess the king and Uncle Yuguro have made the right decision with their plan. There's really no other way.*

Not even the clan chieftains had been informed of Yuguro's grand scheme, for it would shake the country to its very foundations. Most Spears who had participated in the ceremony thirty-five years ago were dead. But if anyone like Laloog, the Yonsa Elder, learned of this plan, they would lay down their lives to prevent it. Which was why members of the older generation, who still revered the Mountain King, must not be told.

Just twenty days to go. If Shisheem did not take his

place, Kahm would accompany his uncle as his attendant in the darkness of the Mountain Deep. Then who would fate favor — the king of Kanbal, or the king under the mountain?

Kahm closed his eyes.

Search parties continued to comb the mountains for the woman, but all trace of her seemed to have vanished at a little hollow on a steep rocky slope. Even after three days, they still had not found her.

The atmosphere in the clan settlement was unusually lively, but Kassa's heart was heavy. On their way back from the great hall, he had accused his father of breaking his promise to defend the woman, but his father only told him that it was for the best.

"You're a man now, so you should remember this lesson well. Master Yuguro made a political decision to protect our clan. We don't need to stir up any more trouble."

Even Kassa understood that much. But still . . .

As he could not talk to his parents, nor tell the truth to his friends, he had no choice but to confide his frustration in the one other person who knew the secret — his sister, Gina.

Out of view among the rocks on the mountain, Kassa told her what had happened in the chieftain's hall. She frowned. "You know," she said, "it seems like one lie just keeps getting added to another."

"That's what I think too, and it makes me feel awful. I can't stand to think the lies started with us."

Gina leaned toward him. "Kassa, we should do something. That woman saved our lives, right? And now she's being hunted because we broke our promise."

"But she's trying to hurt Master Yuguro! And she snuck into the caves to —"

"Just a minute, Kassa," Gina interrupted. "That's what Master Yuguro says, right? But we're the ones who met her in the caves. Shouldn't we consider that? I'd rather decide for myself."

Kassa stared at her in surprise. She was only twelve, but sometimes she impressed him with her logic.

"Don't you think so? We already know what he says isn't always true. So let's think about what we saw before we listen to him. Did she seem like a bad person to you?"

Kassa shook his head.

"You see? And if she really did come for the reason Master Yuguro says, then she could have just ignored our cries for help. If the *hyohlu* had eaten us, there would've been no one to tell on her. I don't know why she came to Kanbal, but whatever the reason, it doesn't change the fact that she risked her life to save us."

Kassa nodded emphatically. For the first time in days his mind felt clear. "You're right," he said. "Gina, you're pretty smart sometimes."

Gina gave a shy, pleased smile.

"But even though it's true, I wonder if we can really do anything to help."

Just then a shrill whistle sounded, surprisingly close. They both jumped as Yoyo poked his face out from behind a nearby rock.

"Kassa, you shouldn't talk so loudly! Sound carries far in such a rocky place. There's a search party over there. If they had heard you, you'd be in big trouble!"

Kassa felt a sudden stab of panic squeeze his chest. "Yoyo! How much did you overhear?"

Yoyo raised his hand in greeting to Gina and then whispered, "Everything. Sorry for eavesdropping, but I had a good reason."

Kassa glared at him. "You're right, we should've been more careful. But what we said was really secret. Please promise you won't tell anyone, not even your own people."

Yoyo scratched his chin, then cocked his head and looked at Kassa. "Listen, do you really feel you owe that woman your lives?"

"Yes!"

"Then will you promise not to betray her ever again?"

Gina answered immediately, "Of course we promise!"

Kassa thought for a minute and then said quietly, "As long as she doesn't harm the Musa clan."

Yoyo looked at Kassa for a moment, as if considering something, and then shrugged his shoulders. "Toto the Elder

is amazing. You both answered exactly as he said you would."
Then he beckoned to them. "Come with me as quietly as you
can. And don't talk."

Kassa and Gina looked at each other and then followed after Yoyo, who had already set off at a brisk pace.
Instead of the winding lateral route that Kassa and Gina
usually used, Yoyo took a narrow track that wove steeply up
between the rocks. *This must be one of the Herder roads*, Kassa
thought. The Herder People knew these high rocky slopes
intimately, including many paths that would seem impassable
to others.

Finally they came to a dead end at the bottom of a huge
rock face. "Here we are," Yoyo said. Gina and Kassa wondered what he meant, as they could see only a thorny shrub
in front of the cliff, but Yoyo rapped a large stone beside the
shrub with his eagle chaser. *Tap, tap, tap.* To their surprise,
the stone rolled forward, as if it were being pushed from
inside. Yoyo's father, Dodo, peered out from the hole. "Are
you alone?"

"Yes, it's all right. I made sure no one followed."

Dodo nodded and looked at Kassa and Gina. "Good.
Kassa, Gina, come inside and watch your step." His face disappeared again. Kassa sat on the edge of the hole and put his
feet inside. Dodo grabbed his legs and lifted him in with sur-
prising strength for such a small man. He pulled Gina in
immediately after, and Yoyo pushed the boulder back into
place from the outside.

"Isn't Yoyo coming?" Kassa asked. From the hollow sound of his voice, he guessed that they must be in a larger space than he had thought.

"No. Someone has to stay outside to replace the stone."

As his eyes adjusted to the dark, Kassa noticed that there was a dim glow in the hollow, cast by a luminous moss growing on the rock.

"Gina, take my hand, and Kassa, you take Gina's." Dodo led them slowly forward, hand in hand. He and Gina did not need to duck as they walked, but Kassa's head brushed the ceiling, so he stooped over. To his surprise, he could feel a faint breeze.

They followed the tunnel beneath the rock and turned right. Instantly, everything grew brighter. Kassa and Gina gasped. The space in front of them could have sat about ten adults. Directly before them ran a long horizontal crack, about the width of Kassa's head, where several large rocks came together. Through it shone a blinding ray of sunshine. The fresh breeze Kassa had sensed wafted through the crack, keeping the air in the cave fresh. A woman sat beside it, leaning against the wall. Although her back was to the light, they recognized her immediately as Balsa.

"Hello there." She raised her hand in greeting.

Kassa stood frozen in shock. "Um, I," he stammered, his voice catching in his throat.

Before he could finish, Gina blurted out, "We're so sorry! We told our parents about you. We didn't mean to, but you see, there was a piece of *luisha*, I guess it must have fallen from the *hyohlu*, and —"

Someone grabbed her hand and she jumped. "Hold your horses," Toto the Elder whispered. He had been sitting right beside her and she had not even noticed. "Not so loud now. See that window over there? Your voices carry outside."

Gina and Kassa took turns explaining why they had broken their promise. Balsa smiled faintly, but when they had finished, she nodded. "I see. Well, I suppose I lied a little as well, so let's just say we're even."

Kassa and Gina sighed. Their legs were trembling.

"Don't just stand there. Have a seat." Toto gave Kassa a shove and the two of them sat down on a dry rock.

"You're Kassa and Gina, right? Let me introduce myself properly. I'm Balsa Yonsa, daughter of Karuna from the Yonsa clan."

Kassa, calmer now, took a closer look at Balsa's face. Her skin was tanned and a few fine lines crinkled at the corners of her eyelids. But it was the intensity of her eyes and the frankness of her gaze that truly caught his attention.

"Are you injured?" Gina asked, noticing the cloth bandage binding her left shoulder.

Before Balsa could respond, Toto said, "She was grazed by a poisoned spearhead. *Togal.* As I'm sure you know, we use it against the eagles, so we also know the antidote."

"Yes, and thanks to you the numbness has gone," Balsa

said. "It's sheltered enough in here that I don't need a fire to keep warm, and I've regained much of my strength already with the delicious *laga* and *lakalle*. I don't know how I can repay you."

Kassa frowned. "Weren't you wounded when you fell off your horse?"

Balsa looked puzzled. "No. I didn't fall off a horse. A giant of a warrior threw a spear at me when my back was turned, and I didn't dodge it in time. Shall I show you?"

Casually she removed the cloth to display the ugly wound. Her shoulder had clearly been cut open, and the poison had turned the skin around it a vicious shade of purple.

"They used poison?" Kassa whispered. Had Dom and Kahm poisoned their spear tips? Why would they do that if they were trying to capture her and bring her in for trial? He could think of only one answer to that question. Sickened by the idea, he began to tremble. He mentally went over the words that Master Yuguro had uttered in the great hall. How many lies had he woven into that story? Even if she were a criminal, why had he tried to kill her before she had been given a fair trial by the chieftain?

"Kassa?" Gina's voice jolted him from his thoughts. He wiped the cold sweat from his brow and looked at Balsa.

"Why did you come back to Kanbal?"

Balsa remained silent for some time. Then, with a small sigh, she said, "I came back to Kanbal for a very personal reason — to lay to rest a ghost that haunts me." She smiled briefly. "When I was six, I had to leave Kanbal because of a conspiracy. My father's friend helped me escape. We fled through those caves where I first met you to New Yogo. Twenty-five years have passed since then. The man who raised me died of a sudden illness, but I always felt that he had sacrificed his life for mine, and that thought never left me, no matter how many years passed. So I decided that, instead of trying to ignore this old wound, I would confront it. I chose to go through the same caves that I had been dragged through as a weeping six-year-old, this time relying on my own strength. And that was when I met you."

Kassa frowned in confusion. "Was — was the man who raised you Jiguro?"

Balsa's eyes widened. "How did you know that?"

"Master Yuguro gathered the clansmen and told us. He said that you blamed him for killing Jiguro and you had come here to get revenge."

As understanding dawned on her face, Balsa groaned inwardly. She had expected Yuguro to do all he could to prevent people from finding out about her and Jiguro. It had never occurred to her that Yuguro would tell everyone, even boys such as Kassa, and twist the truth for his own ends. He was much more cunning than she had thought. And he must excel at spinning believable lies.

But she had no intention of telling Kassa and Gina the whole story. They belonged to the Musa clan, and given their innocence, they would find it hard to live among their own people if they knew too much. In fact, she had never intended to involve them at all. She had planned to write a letter to the chieftain and have one of the Herders say they found it in the mountains. In it, she would request a meeting to explain the situation in person.

But Toto pointed out that the men of the clan were convinced that she was a treacherous woman bearing a grudge. Whoever read her letter would see it as a trap. Instead he suggested that she talk to Kassa. He reasoned that as Balsa had saved the boy and his sister, he would feel indebted to her. Both he and Gina were very intelligent, and as children of the chieftain's sister, they would know who in the clan was most trustworthy. Toto insisted that if she wanted to entrust her message to someone, she should meet Kassa, explain at least some of her story, and ask him to take it for her.

But if he already knows about Jiguro, what should I tell him?

Watching her think, Kassa suddenly decided he had had enough. He sensed there was some important secret between this woman and Master Yuguro, and he was tired of being treated like a child, excluded from adult conversation, denied the truth, and brushed off with lies.

"Mistress Balsa! I'm sick of lying and of being lied to. Please tell me the truth. Did you come here to get revenge, to shame Master Yuguro in front of the clan?"

Balsa fixed her piercing gaze on him, then nodded. "When I first came here, I wasn't even thinking of Yuguro. But now, yes, I'd like to pay him back twice over for what he did to me." Her expression was stern. "But not because he killed Jiguro."

"Then why?"

She sighed and shook her head. "I don't want to tell you."

Kassa looked grim. "Then I'll have to tell the chieftain you're here."

Gina stared at her brother in shock. "Kassa!?"

"I can't stand by and let someone harm the clan. I vowed when I received my dagger that I would lay down my life for my people."

Balsa saw the desperation in his eyes and smiled. "I understand. You must do what you feel is right. But at least wait until I'm well enough that I won't get the Herder People in trouble. You owe me that much, don't you think?"

Kassa felt as though she had effortlessly parried a thrust aimed with all his skill and determination. Then another combatant entered the fray.

"Kassa!" Gina said determinedly. "I'm going to stand by Balsa no matter what. And if you try to tell on her, I'll do everything to stop you!"

"Gina, stay out of this!"

"I won't! I'll risk my life to repay what we owe her!"

"Damn it! Can't you see? I don't want to tell on her either. If she would just tell me the truth . . . If she has a good reason, I'll risk anything to help her too."

"Shh! I told you to keep it down." Toto gave each of them a light slap on the head. "Kassa boy, she's just trying to protect you. She doesn't want to bring misfortune on two innocent children by getting you involved. She won't be able to move properly for another day or two, so there's no need to be hasty. Take your time and get to know her a little better before you decide."

Kassa took a deep breath and nodded.

It was almost dusk by the time they came down to the highlands and reached the clan settlement. Gina rushed toward their house, shrieking that she was going to be late helping with supper. Kassa, however, stopped at the sight of a man leaning against the wall of the winter goat pen and gazing absently at the sunset. It was Kahm.

He turned when he noticed Kassa approaching. "Hello there," he said. Kassa dipped his head in greeting and his cousin smiled. "I just dropped in on your mother, but I'm glad I bumped into you. You're the one I really came to see."

Kassa looked up at him in surprise. Kahm was a quiet man with high cheekbones and thick eyebrows, the very image of a warrior. Yet Kassa knew that despite his forbidding appearance, he was very kind. He had often played with Kassa when they were younger, but since his move to the capital a few years ago, they had rarely had a chance to talk.

"You came to see me?"

"Yes." Kahm smiled, embarrassed. The last rays of the setting sun lit up his profile. "Tomorrow I leave for the capital. I wanted to see you before I left . . . because the other day you seemed to be the one person in the great hall who was worried about me."

Kassa's heart ached for him. "How's the injury?"

"Oh, it's fine. It wasn't very serious in the first place."

As he looked at his cousin's profile, Kassa wondered if he had really smeared poison on his spear: Kahm, who more than anyone else hated dishonesty. But he could not ask. Instead he mumbled, "Thank you for coming specially to see me."

Kahm laughed suddenly. Then his face grew serious and he murmured, "Kassa, do you like Kanbal?"

Kassa glanced at him questioningly. "Yes. Why?"

Kahm gazed down on the forests covering the western lowlands. "I've been to other countries, and I know that Kanbal is poor, yet I can't help thinking that it's beautiful too."

Kassa too looked out over the plateau that rolled away to the cliffs and the conifer forests that covered the valley below. He saw what Kahm meant, but he said nothing.

"Soon," Kahm whispered, "the Giving Ceremony will take place. The future of Kanbal rests on the outcome." Still staring at the forests, he continued, "If I should fail to return from the Mountain Deep, I want you to know that I've died because I loved this beautiful land. Be good to my son Kahmuro."

Kassa looked at him in surprise. "But . . . do people die at that ceremony?"

Kahm smiled, but beneath it, Kassa sensed that he was afraid. "I'm only telling you in case, because no one knows what really happens under the mountain." He placed a hand on Kassa's shoulder and shook him gently. "I'm sorry to have bothered you with such foolishness. I'd better be going."

Kassa stayed rooted to the spot, watching his cousin walk away. *What was that all about?* he wondered. It was almost as if Kahm had been giving him his last will and testament. He shivered and kept his eyes fixed on Kahm as he vanished into the darkness.

CHAPTER III
THE HERDERS' SECRET

The longer Balsa spent with the little people called the Herders, the more she became aware of their unusual customs. One day, when a goat was lost in the mountains, she heard them communicating back and forth in a complicated series of whistles.

"What are they saying?" she asked Toto, who spent the whole day tending the fire.

He took a stick of *nyokki* from his mouth. "They're telling each other where the goat is and discussing which path they'll take to bring it down."

"They can say all that just by whistling?"

The old man grinned. "Our whistles are just like words."

Whenever Kassa and Gina climbed up to visit her, which was almost every day, the Herders' signals bounced back and forth. She was sure they were checking to see if the two children were being followed.

In the beginning, Kassa was a little awkward and stiff with her, but as the days wore on, he gradually relaxed. One day when he came to visit, Balsa was practicing on a patch of grass between two rocks. Her spear thrust with blinding speed, to the right, to the left, then spun in a semicircle in a jab to the rear, so that he could almost see her imaginary opponent. He froze, entranced. Her movements were beautiful to watch. Although he had trained with the spear since he was a young boy and had watched many matches, never before had he seen such economy of movement or the speed that turned her spear into a blur of light.

Balsa stopped and turned to look at Kassa. Wiping the sweat from her face, she gave a twisted grin. "Phew! I'm so out of shape! I'm not going to be much good if I break into a sweat after only this much practice."

Suddenly she tossed the spear over to Kassa. He grabbed it hastily and Balsa raised her eyebrows. "Go on, show me your stuff. Let me see how Jiguro's nephew wields a spear."

Kassa blushed. He swung it tentatively and was surprised at how smoothly it slid through his hands. The spear and shaft were perfectly balanced. He steadied his breathing, swung the spear whistling once about his head, and leveled it in front of him. Then he launched into a series of moves — thrust, block, and parry.

Well, well, Balsa thought, a little surprised. When she had first met Kassa, she had thought he lacked courage, but with a spear in his hand, he was bold and confident. She could tell that he loved what he was doing, and her experienced eye saw the makings of an excellent spear-wielder. If Jiguro were still alive, if he had never had to leave Kanbal, he would have helped Kassa develop his talent.

When he finished, Balsa clapped her hands. "Well done! One day, you're going to be a great spearman."

His eyes shone with happiness, but only for a moment. "What's the point of becoming a good spearman when I'm just a warrior from a branch line? I'm going to have to tend goats all my life."

Balsa took the spear back. "So you only train in case of emergencies, is that it? But have you ever thought that you're actually very lucky?"

Kassa scowled. "Lucky?"

"Yes. I've had to wield this spear many times even when I didn't want to, just to survive. Sometimes I think how happy I would have been if I'd never had to do that." She swung it whizzing through the air. "But never mind. . . . If I don't get some exercise, I won't be able to wield it at all! Would you be willing to spar with me so I can practice? How about it?"

A slow smile returned to his face.

The days passed pleasantly for Balsa, practicing with Kassa and listening to Gina share rumors from the clan settlement. Balsa felt her suspicions and her anger toward Yuguro sink slowly to the bottom of her mind. Winter was fast approaching. The first snow would probably fall within the next few days. Once the snows came, the Herder People would bring the goats down from the rocky crags and return to the settlement. The rugged grazing lands were no place for men during winter.

Maybe I should go back to Yogo under cover of the snow, Balsa thought as she gazed up at the leaden sky. Her friends there would be glad to see her. And Kassa's technique had improved remarkably in just the few days they had practiced together, so she had taught Jiguro's nephew some of the moves he had drilled into her. Wasn't that enough to make her return to Kanbal worthwhile? What good would it do to take revenge?

If nothing had happened, Balsa would probably have left Kanbal with the first snowfall, never to return. But during those few peaceful days, the weaver of fate was already adding another thread to the cloth.

One night, a piercing whistle split the air. Balsa jolted awake and sat up in her bed in the rock chamber. In the darkness, she could vaguely make out Toto, who had been sleeping on the other side. He rose slowly, unusually tense. "Have we been found?" Balsa whispered.

"No. Something even worse has happened."

After a short interval, Balsa sensed someone else enter the space beneath the rocks. When the small figure emerged from the darkness, however, she was startled. He looked like one of the Herder People, but his eyes glowed green like a wild beast's, and when he moved, he left a trail of light against the blackness.

Not bothering to sit down, he began talking quickly to Toto. To her surprise, he was not speaking Kanbalese. Toto said something and the other responded at length, gesturing at times to emphasize a point. Toto nodded and seemed to give him instructions. The man bowed and left.

"What happened?" Balsa asked. Toto did not answer, but sat motionless in the dark. Finally, she felt him turn toward her. In the faint light from the rock window, she thought she could see his eyes gleaming at her.

"Balsa," he said. "May I ask you a question?"

"Sure."

"Do you feel any loyalty toward Kanbal?"

"Do you mean to the Yonsa clan?"

"Yes, I suppose so."

"Loyalty? No, none. Perhaps I care a little about my native land, but I don't have a trace of the kind of clan loyalty Kassa has."

Toto nodded. "You said that you make your living as a bodyguard, right? That you're paid to protect people?"

She nodded. Toto leaned toward her. "Can I hire you to do a job then?"

Balsa pulled back, frowning. "Why? Who on earth could you want me to protect?"

"It's a tangled ball of yarn, as we say here. The story's so complicated it will take a while to explain. And to do that, I'll have to break one of the laws of my people. But there's no point in obeying the rules if it means we lose everything else. Balsa, rest for another thirty *lon*. When I wake you, put on your *kahl* and your boots and follow me. I'm going to take you to our meeting place."

Balsa sensed danger ahead, but she owed the Herder People. Although she did not understand what was happening, she could not desert them in a crisis.

Kassa felt someone shaking him and woke with a start.

"Kassa," Gina whispered in his ear. Her teeth were chattering. "Wake up. Nahna's waiting."

"Nahna?" Kassa repeated sleepily. Nahna was a Herder — Yoyo's mother.

"She threw a stone through the smoke hole to wake me up and told me to get you. She's outside. She said to be sure you wear your *kahl*."

Kassa rubbed his eyes and hastily pulled his boots from under the bed. The freezing air struck him as soon as he threw off the covers. Shaking with cold, he got ready.

"She said I couldn't come," Gina continued. "Kassa, do you think something's happened to Balsa?"

"I don't know. Anyway, I'll go see. Hurry up and get back into bed. You'll catch a cold like that."

Kassa felt Gina's anxious eyes on him. Taking her by the shoulders, he gave her a gentle nudge. "Off you go now. It'll be all right. No matter what happens, I'll stand by Balsa." He felt the tension drain from her body.

He lowered the rope, climbed down from the smoke hole, and ran over to Nahna. Her eyes gave off a green light, and he started when he saw her face.

"Master Kassa. Toto the Elder needs you. Come with me. I'll take you to Eagle's Nest."

"Eagle's Nest? Now?" Kassa exclaimed. Eagle's Nest was halfway up the crags and so steep and rugged that not even the mountain goats approached it. Kassa had never been there, but he was sure it would be impossible in the pitch dark.

"Don't worry. I'll guide you. But hurry."

"Wait. I need to get a torch."

"No torches. People will see us. It's all right. Give me your hand and I'll show you the way."

Nahna was so short she only came up to Kassa's navel, but she moved very quickly. He ran after her through the dark.

Balsa woke after sleeping for about an hour and followed Toto outside. Although her night vision was comparatively good, it was still difficult to climb the rocks just by the light of the stars. Thorny shrubs growing between the stones scratched her hands as she hurried after the Elder, who moved as nimbly as if it were midday. Suddenly he seemed to vanish between two rocks. A second later she heard his muffled voice. "The path slopes a long way down here. Be careful not to slip."

The crevice slanted steeply downward and was barely high enough for her to crouch inside: It would have been impassable for a grown man. Still crouching, she worked her way along it for some time before her feet finally touched level ground. She ducked under the edge and came out into a strange grassy field. Massive rocks towered on every side, as if they were at the bottom of a deep bowl. A light flickered at the foot of the west wall. Beckoned by Toto, Balsa stepped onto the grass, but then stopped dead. She sensed others there — not just one or two, but a huge crowd. Yet when she looked around, she saw no one, just the tall black stones looming in the darkness.

"Come to the fire. I thought you might find it too cold here, so I lit one for you."

A warm flame wavered above a pat of dried goat dung in the middle of a simple fire pit. Balsa sat down beside it and wrapped her *kahl* tightly about her.

"Let me share with you one of Kanbal's secrets," Toto said quietly. Perhaps due to the shape of the space, his voice echoed up the stone walls. "There are two kingdoms in the Yusa mother range: the kingdom above ground, which is ruled by the king of Kanbal, and the kingdom beneath, which is ruled by the Mountain King. We, the Herder People, once belonged to the kingdom below."

Balsa breathed in sharply.

"We used to travel freely back and forth between the two kingdoms." Toto spread his arms. "That's why we're so small. And we know how to see in the dark."

He stood up and walked behind the fire pit. Balsa saw him bend down and take something from where the grass met the rock. He returned with a small leaf from which hung a drop of water. "Close your eyes." She did as she was told and felt the cold leaf brush her eyelids. "Now open them."

She opened her eyes and gasped. The world was transformed. Everything glowed bluish-white, as if bathed in moonlight. Even the hollows in the stones were lit up in stark relief. And crouching on the walls that towered above her, the Herder People stared down at her, like birds perched on rocky ledges.

"This has happened before," she whispered. "When I was poisoned — when I saw the Titi Lan, everything looked bright, just like this."

"That's right. This is a *togal* leaf. If you boil a few of these down, you can make a deadly poison. But a drop from a leaf soaked in water isn't poisonous. Long ago, we could see in the dark without this, but we spent so many years in the sunlight that we gradually lost our night vision. The Titi Lan, and others like them, still live in the caves under the mountains. It's too bright for them outside during the day."

He sat down at the edge of the fireplace and Balsa narrowed her eyes. The light from the flames was so intense that she could not look at him directly.

"I don't know when we first began to live above ground, but it was long, long ago. The people of Kanbal were very poor. Sometimes they found precious gems in the river. Assuming that there must be a huge hoard of jewels under the mountain, they decided to invade. Unlike the world above, however, the land below was in utter darkness. Many Kanbalese perished there in the dark, dyeing its waters red with blood.

"A few men of greater mettle survived. When they saw the Mountain King, they realized just what they had pitted themselves against and begged forgiveness. The King pardoned them and promised to send *luisha* every few decades to these poor brothers who lived above ground. They thanked him and vowed that when they came to receive his precious gift, they would prove their sincerity to the Mountain King. This was the beginning of the Giving Ceremony.

"Our ancestors originally lived in the caves near the surface and worshipped the Mountain King. To the Kanbalese, however, we only showed ourselves as the Herder People, who tend the mountain goats on the crags. We hid the fact that we were subjects of the Mountain King in order to keep an eye on them. They're a very hasty, greedy people. We were afraid that someday they might break their promise and again stain the land below with blood."

Toto smiled suddenly. "But after so many years of living with them, we gradually came to love them. Now we think of them as our friends. They may be foolish and hasty, but they are also a kind, warmhearted people. We don't interfere with their lives out under the sun. But if any of them should wander like a lost goat into the caves with some foolish idea of stealing the stones, it's our duty to stop them."

Balsa could only stare at Toto speechlessly as he related this tale. He grinned. "Some among the Kanbalese know our secret. And they hold us in great esteem. . . . Your foster father, Jiguro, was one of these."

"What?"

"He was a great Dancer, you know."

"Dancer?"

"The one who partners the *hyohlu* in the Spear Dance. Only the best spear-wielder is chosen for this honor.

"At the time of the Giving Ceremony, the greatest warriors from each clan — the King's Spears and their attendants — descend beneath the mountain. They compete with each other, and the one who emerges victorious dances with the *hyohlu*, who guards the Last Door. When the *hyohlu* acknowledges the Dancer as the victor, the door finally opens, and the true form of the Mountain King is revealed. That is when the men of Kanbal learn for the first time who we, the Herder People, really are."

Toto sighed. "I knew Jiguro from the time he was born. He didn't show his feelings much, but he was a solid, honest man. And he was a gifted spearman, far surpassing any other from his youth. It didn't surprise me one bit that he beat all the Spears to become the Dancer, even though he was just an attendant. Still . . ." He stopped and stared steadily at Balsa. "His gift brought disaster to Kanbal."

"That's not —" Balsa began, but he raised his hand.

"I know. He was forced to make that decision in order to save your life. But it still doesn't change the fact that he brought great misfortune to this land." He gazed at her with piercing eyes. "Yuguro claims that before he died, Jiguro chose him to succeed him as the King's Spear. Even if he lied about defeating Jiguro, is it true that Yuguro was chosen as the Spear?"

Balsa shrugged. "How should I know? All I know is that they practiced together in the dead of night, and when he left, Jiguro gave him his gold spear ring."

Toto nodded. "If Jiguro, the last Dancer, gave his ring to Yuguro, it means that he wished him to become the next Dancer. Jiguro brought much unhappiness to Kanbal, but that was the seed of the worst evil."

"What do you mean?"

Toto looked at Balsa with glittering eyes. "You think that Jiguro killed his friends. But that's because he couldn't say more. Like all those who have been to the Mountain King's palace, he vowed to remain silent for life about what he had witnessed there." Toto moistened his lips. "Let me tell you how the ceremony works. If you think about why youths of only sixteen or seventeen are allowed to attend when it's supposed to be for the strongest spear-wielders in Kanbal, you'll understand why he did something much worse than just killing his friends.

"Up until now, this ceremony was held about once every twenty years. To participate more than once, a man would have to be under twenty-five the first time he went as an attendant or a Spear, because by forty-five he'd be reaching his limit as a spear-wielder. The first Spears, who knew just how difficult, how terrifying, the ceremony was, made sure that at least some of the participants would be experienced enough to prevent failure. They started the custom of bringing attendants so that nine participants were always young enough to participate in the next ceremony."

The stern light in Toto's eyes sharpened. "Now do you understand? All the young men that Jiguro killed had served either as a Spear or as an attendant in the last ceremony thirty-five years ago. In other words, Jiguro slew all those who might have become the Dancer in the next ceremony."

A shiver ran up Balsa's neck.

"The king called Rogsam was a terrible man. Not only did he kill his older brother to seize the throne, but he also found the perfect excuse to eliminate the best young men from every clan . . . Jiguro."

Balsa felt her body go numb. What an appallingly clever trap Rogsam had hidden within the lie that made Jiguro a thief. And Jiguro had played right into his hands.

"Rogsam was probably aiming to weaken the clans and make his rule as king absolute." Toto shook his head. "But he lacked a vital piece of information. He had never seen the Giving Ceremony. It was his older brother Naguru who had served as the king's attendant, so he didn't know what it meant to wipe out all future candidates for the Dancer."

Toto suddenly brought his face up close to Balsa's. "I'm the eldest of my people. Though I have only a few years left to live, I still receive all messages and make all final decisions. We've known that something was afoot for some time now. Tonight I received word from the Herders who live in the mountains near the capital, confirming that our fears were well founded. Yuguro and the current king of Kanbal have hatched an incredibly foolish plot."

He sighed deeply and then said with disgust, "When the Last Door opens at the ceremony this year, Yuguro and King Radalle plan to invade the palace of the Mountain King with an army of several hundred men. They aim to conquer the land beneath the mountain and take as much *luisha* as they want." A mixture of sorrow and anger kindled in his eyes. "If only Jiguro hadn't killed those young men. None of the king's men went below in the last ceremony. They have no idea what a stupid, futile dream this is. The king might be a fool, but if his Spears were wise and steady, such a plan wouldn't even have been considered."

His gleaming eyes bored into Balsa. "The Darkness within the caves reads the minds of men. If the *hyohlu* detect any enmity toward the Mountain King in the heart of the Dancer, they'll kill him instantly. No matter how great a warrior he may be, nothing can stop them if they wish to destroy him. And even if thousands of soldiers could be hidden in the Mountain Deep, they could never defeat the *hyohlu*."

Balsa shivered again, remembering the cleanly sliced torch in the cave.

Clenching his teeth, Toto the Elder declared emphatically, "When hostility fills the Darkness of the ceremony chamber, this country will fall. If the *hyohlu* kills the Dancer, the Last Door will not open. If the door fails to open, Kanbal will have no *luisha*. Without *luisha*, there will be no grain. Without grain, thousands will die of hunger." He closed his eyes. "How I wish I had never lived to see such things as this."

159

Silence filled the darkness. Not a breath was heard.

Balsa shook herself as if to throw off the weight of that silence. "And just what are you trying to make me do?"

Toto looked up. "I want you to protect Kassa."

"You what?" Balsa frowned. She could not see how his tale was related to Kassa.

Toto leaned toward her. "There's only one way to save Kanbal. The king and his Spears must be convinced to give up their plan before the *hyohlu* enter the chamber."

"Surely you're not planning to make Kassa do that? That's crazy! How can you possibly expect him to convince the king or anyone else?"

"Let me finish, will you?" Toto snapped irritably. "Believe me, I know full well how risky this is. But I can't think of any other way. If more of those who were at the last ceremony still lived, I wouldn't even consider it. Anyone who has been below would listen to us. They'd understand the consequences of trying to attack the Mountain King." His eyes glittered brightly. "But they're all dead. Even those who weren't killed by Jiguro have died over the last thirty-five years. Only two remain: Laloog of the Yonsa clan and Lonsa of the Muto clan. Of course, the best thing would be for them talk to the king and his men in person, but they're so old, they're too weak to walk. And even by horse, it's a ten-day journey from Yonsa and Muto territory to the chamber."

Toto struck the ground twice. "We know a road underground by which you can reach the place in just four days. But while it's easy for little people like us, there are places where it's too narrow for the men of Kanbal to pass."

Balsa grimaced. She was beginning to see why the Elder had picked Kassa.

"As you've guessed, Kassa's small. And you too are much smaller than many men. The two of you could travel this road and reach the ceremony in time. Laloog of the Yonsa clan is highly respected by all the clans because he went to the last ceremony. If Kassa takes a message from him, some men will listen —"

"Are you out of your mind?!" Balsa burst out. "Neither the king nor Yuguro will give up this plan now that they've set it in motion! Kassa will be caught and killed! He's only fifteen. How can you think of risking his life —"

"That's why I'm asking you to protect him. Fortunately the chamber where the ceremony takes place is very dark. If they refuse to change their minds, you can take Kassa and flee."

Balsa glared at him, but he did not avert his gaze. "No matter how great the risk, it's the only way to save Kanbal. Won't you help us?" Once again, he brought his face up close to hers. "Balsa, Spear Wielder, trained by the Dancer Jiguro, when you returned to Kanbal, the *hyohlu* came up from the Mountain Deep to dance with you. Never has such a thing happened before. And you were rescued by the Titi Lan and so brought to us." He smiled broadly. "Surely this can't have been coincidence. Jiguro, though chosen, betrayed the Mountain King and brought great misfortune on his native land. He slew our young spearmen and gave his gold ring to Yuguro. Even if he did it out of love for his brother and for the sake of the chieftain's line, how can his soul ever find peace in death?"

Balsa gritted her teeth as the words Jiguro had uttered on his deathbed rang once again in her mind. *I'll sink beneath the Yusa mountains, the mother range, and atone for my sins myself.*

"Don't you see, Balsa? It must be fate that brought you here, so that you, who were trained by Jiguro, should risk your life for Kanbal."

Balsa looked at him sharply. "Don't be a fool!" Clenching her teeth, she almost snarled the words at him. "All this country ever gave me were days full of hell. Jiguro brought you misfortune? And who do you think made him do that? I will never believe that Jiguro was wrong. He made the only choice he could. If I were given the same choice, I would do the same thing. How dare you dismiss our lives, all those days of suffering, as 'fate'!"

Toto recoiled as if he had been struck in the face.

Balsa breathed deeply and struggled to get her feelings under control. Finally she said in a low voice, "If, just *if*, I should gamble my life on anything, it will not be for Kanbal.

It will be for Jiguro, who suffered a living hell until the day he died for the sake of this country."

Toto remained silent for some time staring at Balsa. Then he spoke. "All right. For Jiguro then. But will you do it?"

Balsa shook her head. "No."

"Balsa!"

"Enough! Jiguro has already been forced to live through this hell by 'fate,' as you would have it. One person is enough. I will not let Kassa repeat the same mistake!"

Her voice split the air like a crack of thunder. When the echo finally faded, a thin voice rang out from above.

"I'll go."

Balsa turned around in surprise. A shadow on the east wall stood up. Helped by another figure, he picked his way awkwardly to the grassy floor.

"Kassa . . ."

Togal flickered in his eyes. Balsa turned back to Toto. "You let him listen to all that?"

The Elder's face grew stern. "Balsa. You're forgetting something very important. This isn't your problem; it's Kassa's. And the success or failure of this venture is much more important to Kassa than it is to you. It's Kassa and his people, not you, who will starve if they get no *luisha*."

Balsa looked once again at Kassa. His face was desperately determined. Since Nahna had led him here, he had sat on the rock shelf, sandwiched between the Herder People, who kept him warm, and listened to what was being said below. When he heard about his uncle Yuguro's scheme, he remembered the words Kahm had said to him the other evening. To gain control over the kingdom beneath the mountains and take all the *luisha* they wanted: This was the dream of every Kanbalese. But as he listened to Toto's tale, he had begun to shiver with apprehension. A premonition that Kahm and the others were about to make a terrible mistake — a mistake that could never be made right — grew stronger. Kahm must have felt this too. Why else would he have left Kassa with words that sounded like a last will and testament?

He did not want Kahm to die. And as for famine . . .

He shuddered. He found it hard to grasp the weight of the responsibility being thrust upon his shoulders. He looked up at Balsa, feeling like he was dreaming. "I'll go. Even if I have to go alone."

Looking at his face, Balsa felt fear rise from deep in her chest. As a bodyguard, she had been entrusted with the lives of many others, but never had she been afraid like this, not even when she had protected Prince Chagum, the Guardian of the Spirit. Chagum had had no other choice. And so she had believed that she too had no choice but to risk her life along with him and find a way through.

But this boy was choosing to gamble his life on her of his own accord. . . .

"It's just me against the best spearmen in Kanbal," Balsa muttered. "The odds are so great. . . . I may not be able to save your life. Do you realize what will happen to you then?"

Kassa nodded.

"Do you still want to go?"

"Yes," he whispered. "I don't want to watch my people die."

PART 4
FACING THE DARKNESS

CHAPTER I
LALOOG THE ELDER

Laloog was dozing on the couch when Mistress Yuka came to visit. The events of the past few days had left him exhausted. His younger son, Luke, was the current chieftain of the Yonsa clan, and when he heard that the Gate to the Mountain Deep had opened, he immediately sought his father's advice. As one of the last participants of the previous Giving Ceremony and Elder of the Yonsa clan, Laloog was highly revered. But inwardly, he was exasperated that his son insisted on consulting him about everything from the gifts for the Mountain King to the hospitality that should be offered to the envoys from the capital.

Yesterday they had finally sent off the carts, heavily laden with gifts, and, at last, fatigue overtook the old man. He had found it hard even to get out of bed this morning. He felt himself drawing closer to death a little at a time, but he supposed it could not be helped. After all, he had never expected to live to seventy.

He woke to a knock on the door, but it was a few moments before he could move. "Mmm?" he finally managed to murmur.

"Master Laloog." It was a young guard from the entrance. "Mistress Yuka from the house of healing is here again."

Laloog sighed. "Show her in."

Listening to the young man's footsteps recede into the distance, Laloog stared moodily into the fire. Lately, he dreamed constantly of his eldest son, Taguru, and that could only be due to the unsettling news that Yuka had brought recently. Her words had stirred up the grief that he had thought buried by time. But if what she had told him was true . . .

The moment he had seen her six days ago, he had been filled with foreboding. Nothing unsettled Yuka, not even when she had to lop off a patient's arm, and he had often thought that if she were a man, she would have been an unparalleled warrior. Yet she had rushed into his room with her hair in disarray, and his fears had been immediately confirmed. Greeting him only perfunctorily, she had fixed him with fierce, glittering eyes, and launched into her preposterous tale.

To think that Karuna's daughter still lives . . .

Of course, Laloog had not believed her at first. He had tried to convince Yuka that the woman must have been Jiguro's lover, or that she was manipulating the story of

Karuna's daughter to suit her own designs. But Yuka had merely laughed sharply and shook her head. "It was Balsa," she said. "You'd recognize her too if you saw her."

Laloog had only seen Balsa once before, long ago when Karuna, back from the capital, had paid a visit to Laloog's younger brother, the chieftain. As a Spear, Laloog had also been living in the capital, but he happened to be staying at the chieftain's hall to attend his nephew's coming-of-age ceremony. Karuna had brought his three-year-old daughter with him. Her arm was in a sling, and the white bandage stood out against her skin, which was as darkly tanned as a boy's. Apparently, the first thing she had done on reaching Yuka's house was to fall from a tree and break her arm. "She looks more like Yuka at the same age than you," he had told Karuna.

Those were good years, Laloog thought. *Karuna was the king's physician and we were so proud that he came from the Yonsa clan.*

Then it had all come tumbling down in a landslide of misfortunes — the death of the king, Jiguro's flight, Karuna's murder, and finally the loss of Laloog's eldest son, Taguru, who left in pursuit of Jiguro, never to return. If, as Yuka claimed, these tragedies had all originated in a plot hatched by King Rogsam . . .

Laloog recalled King Rogsam's oily face, and then the face of Jiguro Musa as a youth of sixteen, shining with courage in the Darkness below. He felt as if Jiguro, a man he had hated and tried hard to forget these many years, had suddenly fixed his fearless, determined eyes on him.

He came back to the present at the sound of the door opening. The pungent smell of rubbing ointment preceded Yuka into the room. She came every day on the pretext of treating the pain in his joints.

When she met his eyes, he shook his head gently. "They haven't caught her yet."

Rumor had swept through the Yonsa and Musa clans faster than galloping horses: The fugitive captured by the two Musa warriors had slipped from their grasp, badly wounding them both. The news had reached Laloog's ears the same day it happened. On its heels came a message from Kaguro Musa himself, officially requesting that the woman be apprehended if she fled into Yonsa territory. Further rumors indicated that a massive search launched by Kaguro had been unsuccessful.

Yuka brought a chair over to Laloog's couch and sat down. She began massaging ointment into his wrinkled elbow with practiced hands. His arm was thin and the muscles were withered, so that the loose, baggy skin moved under her hand each time she ran her fingers over it.

"I hear that Yuguro Musa has already passed through Yonsa territory," she said.

"Yes, he joined up with the men from our clan. They should reach Yonro territory tomorrow."

Yuka increased the pressure in her fingers. "I'm sure Kaguro will listen to you now that Yuguro's gone."

Laloog looked at her sharply. "Yuka —"

"People are saying that Yuguro left Kaguro's eldest son behind and took his own son with him instead. In fact, Master Kahm only passed through Yonsa territory this morning. Surely this is a god-given opportunity. Kaguro must have some misgivings."

Laloog sighed. "You hear everything."

Yuka smiled. "The waiting room at the house of healing has always been a hotbed of gossip."

Laloog gazed up at the ceiling. "You would ask me to trigger an avalanche between the Yonsa and Musa tribes? There's no strength in this old body of mine to stop it once it starts, you know." He added in a whisper, "I can't take that risk on something that won't benefit our clan in any way."

"You are the clan Elder. The clansmen are your children. Would you stand by and watch your children die?" She scooped up some sticky yellow ointment with her ring finger, then said quietly, "Even now I hate the one who killed my brother. I can still see Karuna's dead eyes staring into space. Would you forgive the man who made the best young warriors of our clans die for nothing — the man who sent Taguru to his death?"

Laloog roughly brushed her hand away and sat up with a groan. He faced her, glaring. "Where's the proof? Tell me that. Just where is the proof that will convince our people I should accuse the most powerful man in Kanbal of deception?"

"There is a witness — Balsa. Will you let Yuguro kill her?"

"That's what I mean. There's no proof that that woman is telling the truth." He shook his head. "Yuka, there's nothing I can do about it. How many times are you going to bring this up?"

She stared straight into his eyes. "As many times as it takes. Do you think I'm going to stand by and let him kill my only niece?"

There must be some way to help Balsa. This thought consumed Yuka both waking and sleeping. But she always came back to that one fatal flaw: There was no way to prove that Balsa was telling the truth.

When she left Laloog's room and went outside, snow was falling like dust from the silver sky. The men were busy fixing the winter livestock pens to ready them for the goats being herded down from the crags. Soon the mountains would be buried in snow.

Yuka wondered where Balsa was now. Mounting her short, sturdy mare, she headed back to the house of healing through a flurry of powdery flakes.

That night Laloog heard a strange bird calling him in his dreams. He opened his eyes with a start and lay on his bed listening to the faint sound of the wind. The room was dark. The fire had died down to embers that cast only a feeble glow.

Suddenly, he tensed. Through the chimney came a high, thin whistle. When he grasped its meaning, he began to tremble. Thirty-five years ago he had heard that same call in the Mountain Deep: *"The People of the Mountain King have come to speak to thee."*

He lay motionless in stunned disbelief. But when he heard it again, he rose from his bed and dressed warmly in seldom-used boots, two pairs of woollen socks, and his thick *kahl.* Then he went over to the window and opened it as quietly as possible.

A cold, snowy gust blew into the room. The window faced onto the back garden, which was sunk in darkness, but below the windowsill he saw two small bluish-white eyes glowing in the black.

"Welcome, Servant of the Mountain King," Laloog said in a low voice. "Please come in."

The villages of Kanbal bustled with activity during Langal Tonoi, the month of the first snow, when the Herders brought the goats down to their winter pens beside the clan settlement. Herder men and boys lived much of the year in simple huts beside the high mountain pastures, while the women lived in houses just outside the village, working in the fields and weaving. But at the beginning of winter, all the clansmen helped tend the goats, and the clanswomen likewise took over the Herder women's share of the fieldwork, knowing they were busy welcoming their menfolk home.

Kassa too was swept up in the activity. As he gathered his family's goats, he watched Toto the Elder, Yoyo, and the others joyfully returning to their homes just outside the outer wall of the village. He found it hard to believe that the people rejoicing at this homecoming were the same ones who had crouched with him on the rock shelves only a few nights before.

While it was a season of reunion for the Herder People and their families, it was also the time when most clansmen left their families to seek work in New Yogo. The men's well-worn *kahls*, painstakingly waterproofed with grease, hung from the eaves of the clan's houses, swaying in the wind over small mounds of earth: the graves of the countless children who had died soon after birth. In a poor country like Kanbal, only four out of every ten children survived. Those who died were buried in the shelter of the eaves, where they became guardian spirits watching over the house. The *kahls* were hung over their graves in hopes that their spirits would slip inside the cloaks, protecting their fathers or brothers on their journeys to foreign lands.

Children now sat by these same graves, rubbing grease into the men's boots. They talked and laughed with their friends as their fingers worked the leather. They would miss their fathers and brothers during the long winter months, but they accepted their temporary absence as part of life. Nor did the men who would soon be leaving appear sad or gloomy. Working in foreign lands far from their families was hard, but for the young ones, it was also a chance to see the outside world and learn from their elders how to find a little fun. For the older men, it was simply what they did every winter.

Kassa's father had at first been happy that he could stay home, thanks to the large sum of money they'd received for the *luisha*. But when he saw his fellow villagers preparing to go, he spent much of that small fortune buying new boots for all of them, probably out of guilt. Driving the goats along the path, Kassa overheard several men talking about Tonno's gift as they fixed a fence. "It was nice of him," they said with affection and a trace of humor. "But how like Tonno to worry about what others might think!" Kassa listened with mixed feelings, understanding both the men's thoughts and his father's motivations.

As Kassa herded the disgruntled goats into the enclosure, he glanced toward the village gate. According to Toto, the Yonsa clan Elder should arrive sometime today. "Ow!" he yelped as a goat stepped on his foot. He blushed, embarrassed, but fortunately no one else seemed to have noticed.

Just then the shrill blast of a horn split the air. Kassa jumped and looked toward the gate again. Far in the distance, he saw people coming up the road from the valley. A warrior rode ahead, the Yonsa flag tied to his spear flapping in the wind, and behind him rolled a horse-drawn carriage accompanied by a single horseman.

He's here. The Yonsa Elder really had come to meet Kaguro, just as Toto had said. The village was now astir with excitement at their arrival. As he pushed an escaping goat back into the pen, Kassa hoped with all his heart that the meeting would go well.

Frowning slightly, Kaguro came out to greet his unexpected guest. Guards lined both sides of the road from the gate to the hall as the carriage, flanked by two mounted warriors, drew up to the entrance. As soon as it halted, a strange woman wrapped in a *kahl* climbed out quickly and then turned to help Laloog down. She led him forward to stand before the Musa chieftain.

"Master Kaguro," Laloog said in a rasping voice. "Please forgive me for arriving unannounced."

Kaguro inclined his head slightly. "No, no, you are welcome," he said. "Please come inside. We'll prepare a feast to celebrate your visit." He turned to lead his guest toward the great hall.

"Just a moment, Master Kaguro. I've actually come to discuss something highly confidential."

Kaguro paused, momentarily discomfited. As one of the last surviving Spears, Laloog was held in high esteem by all the clans, and Kaguro felt a little nervous in his presence. "Ah, I see. Then shall we go to my private chamber?" He led him deeper into the building to his room. He noticed that although Laloog had claimed the discussion was to be confidential, he showed no sign of dismissing the woman by his side.

Once the three were alone in the dimly lit, chilly room, Kaguro hastily added coals to the fire and stirred up the flames. Then he led Laloog over to an armchair. After a brief glance at the woman, he looked at Laloog. "Excuse me, but who is this?"

Laloog returned his gaze steadily. "Let me introduce you. This is Balsa of the Yonsa clan, daughter of Karuna, and Jiguro's foster child."

Kaguro reeled backward as if he had been struck. Quietly removing her *kahl*, Balsa turned to him and bowed slightly.

"Wha — what do you mean by this?" After the first shock of surprise, anger kindled in Kaguro's eyes. "This woman is a criminal, one I requested you *capture* to protect the honor of my clan! Why have you —"

Laloog raised his hand abruptly. "Master Kaguro. Will you trust me long enough to hear me out?"

Kaguro clenched his shaking fists and sat down heavily in a chair.

"It's a long story — and a disturbing one. But the fate of Kanbal rests upon whether or not you choose to believe me. So please listen carefully." Quietly but passionately, Laloog began relating the tale of Balsa's father, Karuna, physician to King Naguru, of his friendship with Jiguro, and of Rogsam's treacherous plot. . . .

Kaguro sat rigidly as he listened to the dark tale unfold. Partway through, Balsa picked up the thread and in her pleasantly low, calm voice related what had transpired after their flight from Yogo. By the time she reached her return to Kanbal, the last rays of the dying sun had already faded into blackness.

When she finished, Kaguro remained motionless for some time. Finally he raised his face and looked at Laloog, his eyes gleaming. "What proof do you have that this story is true?"

Laloog gave a small sigh. "Only that this woman is truly Karuna's daughter, Balsa. That I can guarantee. My healer, Yuka, was Karuna's younger sister — in other words, Balsa's aunt — and if you saw her, one glance would convince you that they are indeed blood kin."

"But —"

Laloog cut him off before he could speak. "As I explained, Karuna told Yuka that Balsa died in an accident, then he himself was murdered only days later. Yuka's a physician. She saw the marks on her brother's body." He looked up at Kaguro. "I know how flimsy this evidence is. But think, Kaguro. Remember those days. What kind of man was Rogsam? And what kind of man was Jiguro?"

Kaguro bit his lip. The wind seemed to roar in his ears, whipping up the days of his youth, long, long ago. He had been an unremarkable child; his only outstanding talent had been spear-wielding, but even in that he could take no pride because his younger brother Jiguro was always beside him. Jiguro's gift had blossomed at a very young age, and everyone marveled at it, saying that he must have inherited it from his grandfather, who had been chosen as the Dancer.

If Jiguro had been conceited like Shisheem, Kaguro might have hated him. But the more he was praised, the more silent Jiguro became, and the more reluctant to wield his spear in front of others. When he was told that Jiguro had stolen the nine rings and fled in protest against Prince Rogsam's appointment as king, Kaguro had been incredulous. While it was true that Jiguro hated the prince, he had never been one to push his views on others.

Yuguro, however, was the exact opposite. From childhood, he had been bright and cheerful, capable of charming anyone. When Kaguro became chieftain, Yuguro, who was still a youth, had moved to the capital. There he quickly assumed the luxurious life of a city dweller. When he had volunteered to hunt down Jiguro, Kaguro was stunned yet again. He could remember how the usually reticent Jiguro used to pick Yuguro up and play with him when he was just a toddler. Perhaps because he himself was taciturn, Jiguro had been very fond of his gregarious little brother.

And then, when Yuguro returned triumphant, Kaguro felt as though his heart had been gouged from his chest. He knew Jiguro. Yuguro could never have defeated him if Jiguro had fought in earnest, and it grieved him to think he had let his younger brother kill him. Consequently, he found Yuguro's behavior hard to understand. He had slain his own brother, albeit a dishonorable criminal, and won fame and glory as a hero in the capital. If their roles had been reversed and Jiguro had pursued and killed Yuguro, Jiguro would never have shown his face in public again. He would have returned to his village and lived quietly, mourning his brother. . . .

These thoughts churned in Kaguro's mind, clamoring for attention. There was no proof. Yet the man Balsa had just described to him was far more like the Jiguro he had known than the version he had come to believe.

He heaved a great sigh, then looked at Balsa. "And if this story is true, what do you plan to do about it?"

She gazed at Kaguro's lined face. He looked so much more like Jiguro than Yuguro did when she had met him long ago — even the eyes that gazed at her from under slightly furrowed brows.

"Nothing. There's no proof. And besides, nothing I can do will bring Jiguro back to life. If you believe me, then it was worth coming back to let you know your brother was not a traitor, to tell you what kind of life he led." A smile touched the corners of her mouth. "Yuguro tried to poison me, but he didn't need to go to all that trouble. I can't change anything."

Kaguro stood up. "I believe you," he said finally, his voice determined. "But I can't announce that publicly. If you'll promise in writing never to return to Kanbal, you may return freely to New Yogo."

Balsa glanced briefly at Laloog. Three nights ago the Herder People had led her through the caves to Yonsa territory, where Laloog had met her. She had been afraid that Laloog would not believe her tale about the conspiracy, despite his respect for the Herders as people of the Mountain Deep. But on the contrary, he had received her warmly. It was then that she had learned that her Aunt Yuka had been trying to convince him for days.

She turned her gaze back to Kaguro. "I'm afraid that I can't leave Kanbal just yet."

He frowned deeply. "Why not?"

"There's something I have to do."

In response to an urgent summons, Kassa and his father found themselves ushered into Kaguro's private chamber. Kassa, who knew the reason, felt the long-awaited moment had come, but his father, who had no clue of what was going on, looked very anxious. Kaguro, Laloog, and Balsa were waiting for them.

Kaguro greeted them with a deep frown and began methodically explaining the situation. Tonno listened with an expression of stunned disbelief. When he had finished, Kaguro slowly shook his head. "Frankly," he said, "I still can't quite accept it myself." He glanced at Balsa. "I can't help but feel that this idea is too advantageous for you. Protecting Kassa is the perfect excuse for you to sneak into the ceremony chamber and take revenge on Yuguro under cover of the darkness."

Balsa smiled bitterly. "That's true."

"Now wait a minute!" Laloog intervened. "Do you think I would tell such a preposterous lie just to allow Balsa to avenge a grudge?"

Kaguro maintained a sullen silence for a few seconds and then finally sighed. "No . . . When my father was dying, he told me, 'I will make you clan chieftain, but in any matter pertaining to the Mountain King, you must defer to Jiguro because he has seen the King himself. He knows the secret hidden from Kanbal.'" He raised his head and looked at Laloog. "But it never occurred to me that the Herders were people of the Deep . . . or that they were spying on us."

A look of displeasure crossed his face and then faded. "Master Laloog. Even if the tale of the Herder People is true, we're Kanbalese. Shouldn't we be thinking of what will bring happiness to Kanbal? Don't you think Yuguro is right? He's our greatest spearman. Surely there's a chance that he could defeat the *hyohlu*? If his plan should succeed and we gained free access to *luisha* . . ."

Laloog reached out and gripped Kaguro's hand with his own. Surprised, Kaguro looked down at him.

"Master Kaguro. That is a terribly foolish dream. Even now, the fear inspired by the *hyohlu* chills me to the very marrow. As one who has taken part in the Giving Ceremony,

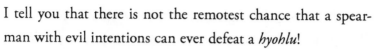

I tell you that there is not the remotest chance that a spear-man with evil intentions can ever defeat a *hyohlu*!

"And know this also. The Mountain King is not what you imagine him to be. I can't tell you what I witnessed beneath the mountain because I'm bound by the vow of silence. But even if I were to try to describe it in words, you'd never be able to understand me."

He squeezed Kaguro's hand tightly. "All I can do is beg you to believe me. *Luisha* is not merely a gem. To invade the Mountain Deep and try to take as much *luisha* as you want is like milking a she-goat to death while demanding that she produce more milk!" His hand was trembling. "When a goat gives birth to a kid, she shares her milk with us. *Luisha* too is a treasure that can only be shared when the time is right."

He gently released Kaguro's hand. "I suppose it's impossible for you to understand how I feel. But Master Kaguro, trust me, for I speak as one of only two men left who have seen the Mountain Deep. If the Mountain King dies, Kanbal will perish with him."

Silence blanketed the room.

Kaguro frowned and looked at Laloog. "But I just can't believe that Yuguro is that stupid. It's true that this time no one has participated in the ceremony before, but Yuguro trav-eled to Yonsa territory to learn all about it from you. Didn't you tell him?"

"Of course I did. I explained everything that happens in the Darkness, but not what happens after the Spear Dance.

That knowledge belongs only to those who participate in the Ceremony." A bitter expression crossed his face as he looked at Kaguro. "You said that you can't believe Yuguro could be so foolish. If I may say so, Yuguro is not a fool, but rather dangerously hard-hearted. His actions have made that abundantly clear, although I've realized it far too late."

Kaguro scowled at him, the cleft between his brows showing starkly. Laloog gazed back steadily.

"As I said, I told Yuguro everything that happens during the ceremony. The fact that he has still gone ahead with this plan means that he didn't take me seriously. And I would wager that he hasn't told the other Spears what he learned from me either." Laloog clenched his fists. "In fact, he has cleverly prevented them from learning anything. My grandson Dahgu has been kept so busy that he hasn't been able to return to Yonsa territory for the last three years. Now I finally understand why."

Anger and fear hung heavy in the room.

"Ex — excuse me . . ." Kassa's father broke the silence. "Forgive me, but surely you can't be suggesting that Kassa try to stop a scheme that clever Master Yuguro has spent so much time planning? Why, that's . . ." He choked and then continued. "That's impossible! I won't let you do that to my son!"

"Father!"

Tonno gestured impatiently for him to be quiet. "If you'll pardon me saying so, even if Master Kahm were to believe Kassa, he has no hope of stopping Master Yuguro either, let

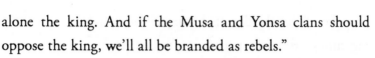

alone the king. And if the Musa and Yonsa clans should oppose the king, we'll all be branded as rebels."

Kassa had never heard his father speak so forcefully. Kaguro and Laloog stared wordlessly at his tanned face, now a dark red as he glared at them. Laloog grimaced and buried his face in his hands. When he lifted it again, everyone was shocked by his expression of despair.

"Then we're lost, for the Darkness reads the minds of men," he said. "When the *hyohlu* comes to the Spear Dance, the chamber is plunged into darkness. Within it wait countless other *hyohlu*, who peer into the hearts of the Kanbalese.

"Experiencing this in the flesh is completely different from hearing it described in words. Yuguro is a master at using words to manipulate people. He probably thinks that he can talk his way through this situation too. But the *hyohlu* aren't so easily swayed. If they sense even a trace of enmity, they'll attack instantly."

The corners of his mouth twisted in a sad smile and his eyes were full of tears. "Yuguro will be slain mercilessly, we'll fail to obtain *luisha,* and Kanbal will starve."

Balsa gazed up at the ceiling with knitted brows. Then, taking a deep breath, she looked down at Laloog and said, "The ceremony chamber, just how big is it?"

He looked up and hesitated, then shrugged his shoulders. "The king, his nine Spears, and their attendants — about twenty people in all — form a circle along the stone walls of the chamber. The spearmen compete in the center of that ring. You'll get an idea of the size if you imagine a space just big enough for twenty men to form a circle."

"So even if there's an army waiting outside, there're only twenty men inside, right? Of those twenty men, how many would side with us if they heard your message?"

Laloog and Kaguro looked at each other. "I suppose Master Kahm and my grandson, Dahgu."

Balsa frowned. "Just two. That's nowhere near enough."

At that moment, Kassa piped up. "Er, excuse me, but . . ." His face flushed beet red as all eyes suddenly turned toward him. He was so nervous that the top of his scalp went numb, but he forged on bravely. "Um . . . The evening before he left for the capital, I met Master Kahm. I don't know how to explain this, but he seemed afraid. He may have been told how the ceremony is conducted, but none of them know what really happens in the Mountain Deep. Master Kahm isn't a coward. I'm sure of that. So it made me think the other warriors must be nervous too." Kassa faced Kaguro, unaware that he was gazing squarely into the eyes of a man he had never had the courage to even look at before.

"Master Kahm told me he was doing this to save Kanbal from starvation, as if he was trying to convince himself that he must risk his life despite his fears. . . . I'm sure that many others must feel the same way. If they're afraid, they just might listen if they hear that I've brought a warning from Master Laloog, who actually knows what happens there."

Tonno was staring at his son as if he were a stranger, but Kassa was so wound up he didn't notice. "I think we have to chance it and hope that others will join us. My father said we might be viewed as rebels, but I don't think this is the time to worry about that. I think it's more like being faced with a herd of goats stampeding toward a cliff. We have to head them off before they go over." He looked at Balsa. "I want to see my cousin Kahm one more time. Please let me go."

Tonno grasped his shoulder. Kassa placed his hand on the hilt of his dagger and looked up at his father. Balsa remained silent, studying the expression on his face. She had thought him cowardly once, but now she saw an unexpected stubbornness. In this state he was likely to go to the Herder People and plead with them to take him even on his own.

She sighed. "Well, if you're that set on it, I suppose we'll just have to give it a try."

Everyone turned to look at her in surprise.

"But in return, Kassa, you must promise me this. If you find that nothing you can do will change things, you must do as I say and run."

Kassa hesitated a moment, but then he nodded.

"Do you promise?"

"Yes."

Balsa looked at Tonno. "I'm still not sure what the inside of that cave is like, but if it's dark, I may be able to help at least Kassa to escape." As she said it, she saw her own death clearly in her mind. But for some reason, the idea of going to the chamber in the Mountain Deep did not bother her. She realized that in her heart she actually wanted to enter that Darkness in which Jiguro had danced with the *hyohlu*.

Tonno looked at her as if he did not know what to do. She gazed back at him. "I can't tell you that I'll bring Kassa back alive," she said. "But I can promise you one thing. I won't return without him."

CHAPTER II
TO THE MOUNTAIN DEEP

Balsa and Kassa left at dawn the next day. Tonno did not tell his family why Kassa was leaving, only that he was being sent by the chieftain on a confidential mission to the capital. Avoiding their worried eyes, he put his hand on Kassa's shoulder and they left the house together.

It was a cold morning. Frost covered the ground and the frozen grass glittered in the light of the newly risen sun. They headed toward the cave where Kassa had first met Balsa. She was already there waiting for them with Kaguro and Toto. To their surprise, even Laloog, the Yonsa Elder, was there, using his spear as a staff. Kassa went to stand silently beside Balsa, his breath turning white in the frosty air. Toto gave each of them a goatskin knapsack.

"There are *togal* and *yukkal* leaves as well as *laga* in these bags. Remember never to light a flame in the caves. You'll be able to see in the dark if you use the *togal* leaves, but there isn't much you can do about the cold. If you can't stand it, eat one of the *yukkal* leaves. They'll warm you up from the inside, and you can rub them on your feet too."

Toto grabbed Yoyo by the elbow. "Yoyo will lead you to the Yonsa clan. Other Herders will be waiting for you in each clan territory. They'll give you more food."

Kaguro stirred. "The ceremony chamber is at the bottom of the cave behind the king's palace. It takes ten days even on horseback to reach the capital from here, but there're only about five days before the ceremony starts. Are you really sure you can make it in time just by traveling underground?"

Toto grinned. "Don't worry. Leave it to us." Then the smile faded from his face and he looked intently at Balsa and Kassa. "When you're in the caves, you may use *togal*. But don't use it after you enter the ceremony chamber. Promise?"

"Why?"

"If you see the *hyohlu*'s true form, you can never return above land."

Kassa felt his father's hand tighten on his shoulder. "Balsa," Tonno said. "Take care of Kassa for me."

She nodded slightly, then turned to Kaguro. "If Kassa should return alive, will you and your clan swear to protect him no matter what happened in the Mountain Deep, no matter the result?"

He gazed steadily back at her. "Anyone born to the Musa clan is the same as my own blood kin. Even if it means

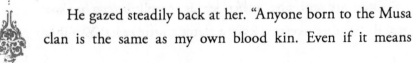

opposing the king, I will never abandon Kassa in order to protect the clan."

Kassa looked up at him in surprise. A stern light gleamed in Kaguro's one eye. He looked down at Kassa and then finally back at Balsa. In an unusually quiet voice, he said, "It's said that in the Darkness under the mountain, men can't hide what is in their hearts. I wonder what Yuguro will see there."

Balsa looked back at him wordlessly. Then with a faint smile she slapped Kassa lightly on the shoulder. "Well, shall we be off?"

He looked up at her and nodded. With Yoyo in the lead, they stepped into the dark cave.

"Make sure you come back!" Tonno yelled after them. His voice bounced off the walls, gradually fading into silence.

When the three figures had disappeared from sight, Kaguro turned abruptly from the cave entrance and stalked away. Toto the Elder fell in step alongside Laloog.

"Do you think Balsa will succeed?" Laloog whispered.

Toto glanced up at him. Only he and Laloog knew the secret that they had not shared even with Balsa and Kassa, let alone Kaguro and Tonno. "She will. I believe it was fate that brought her here, although she was furious with me for using that word 'to dismiss her suffering,' as she put it. But sometimes things seem connected by a strange thread that pulls them all together. You know what I mean?" He smiled slightly. "At least, that's what I felt when I heard that a *hyohlu* had not only met Balsa on her way through the caves, but danced the Spear Dance with her and gave Gina a piece of *luisha*. And now look. In the winter that Balsa and the *hyohlu* met, the ceremony is finally about to take place, after a delay of fifteen years."

Laloog stopped walking abruptly. A sad light gleamed in his eyes. He whispered gently, "I see . . . You mean the *hyohlu* was waiting for Balsa?"

Toto nodded. "I think so. This ceremony is special. Though the king of Kanbal and his Spears don't know it, this ceremony must cleanse the people of Kanbal of Rogsam's sins. His scheming warped and twisted Balsa's life, and the suffering he caused affected her perhaps most of all. Could there be anyone more suited to purifying this rite than Balsa?"

He looked up at Laloog and lightly touched his hand. "And who better than she to lay to rest the Guardians of the Darkness, who were also tainted? So, Laloog, let's pray that Balsa succeeds in washing away these sins and giving them peace at last."

Balsa and the others walked silently until the light behind them dwindled to a white dot. When the light disappeared completely, they stopped to moisten the *togal* leaves with drops of condensation from the wall and brush them against their eyelids.

Kassa opened his eyes and gasped in surprise. The white *hakuma* walls now sparkled around them. He noticed holes here and there in the stone. "What are those?" he asked Yoyo.

"The houses of the Titi Lan, the Ermine Riders," Yoyo whispered. "Kassa, don't talk so loud. The people who live here have just gone to bed. And don't tap your spear on the floor as you walk either. Sound carries along the rock walls."

Kassa hastily slung his spear on his shoulder. The *hakuma* stretched before him like a corridor of snow. The caves were much bigger than he had ever expected. When he looked up, the roof was so high he could not see where the space ended, and the branches opened up in countless directions. Yoyo pressed ahead without hesitation, and Kassa wondered what he was using as landmarks. He and Balsa had already completely lost track of which direction they were heading. If they were separated from Yoyo now, death would be their only exit.

Balsa rubbed her finger over the mark on her spear. Judging by the fact that she had seen the same mark on Kaguro's, long ago the Herder People must have taught someone from the Musa clan the route through the caves to New Yogo. *What drove that first wanderer to travel there?* she wondered as she walked along.

After a while, the walls began to glow a light green. *"Lyokuhaku,"* Kassa murmured. Up to this point, they had walked through a deep silence broken only by the sound of their footsteps, but now they could hear the sound of running water.

"This branch road is quite narrow, so be careful," Yoyo said as he bent over at the waist to duck inside. Balsa and Kassa got down on all fours and somehow managed to crawl through.

When they came out on the other end, Balsa caught her breath. A vast river flowed in front of her at alarming speed, carving away the luminous pale-green walls and lapping against the ledge on which she knelt. "It's so deep," Kassa gasped in fright, gazing down into the water. Balsa looked over the edge and a chill went up her spine. The water was crystal clear, and though she could see a long way down, she

could not see the bottom. Shimmering with a pure green light, it was both breathtakingly beautiful and absolutely terrifying.

"Yoyo, what are we going to do?" Kassa asked. "You're not expecting us to swim through that, are you?"

Yoyo laughed. "Of course not. Put your hand in it and you'll see. The water's as cold as ice. If you fell in there, you'd be dead before you knew it. Just be patient a minute."

He began whistling. The high sound echoed off the walls, reverberating through the cave. Before it faded, he pulled some *yukkal* leaves from his bag. The pungent odor stung their noses.

"Take off your boots, and your socks too. Then knead some leaves and rub them against your legs like this." He

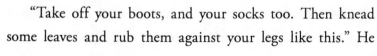

rubbed the juice from the leaves into his skin, starting from his toes and traveling all the way up to just below the knee.

They did as they were told and felt heat spreading up their legs. "Hey, it's really hot! Are you sure it's all right?"

Yoyo grinned and pulled on his socks and boots. "Believe me. You'll soon be more than grateful for that warmth. . . . Look. It's here."

They followed the direction of his finger and stared in astonishment. An enormous, slender creature was weaving its way up toward them from the river depths. It was the strangest thing Kassa had ever seen. At first, it looked like an eyeless snake, but then he saw its pectoral fins paddling through the water like legs. Its body glowed with a faint, pearlescent luster. Two large airholes at the tip of its pointed face stayed closed under water, but when it surfaced, they opened with a shrill whistle.

Yoyo whistled again for what seemed a long time. As if in answer, the creature huffed from its airholes. Then Yoyo took out a lump of dried goat meat and threw it. With a loud splash, the creature caught it in jaws lined with sharp teeth and gobbled it up. "Sootee Lan, Rider of the Water Currents, will carry us to Yonsa territory," Yoyo said as he casually climbed on its back.

Balsa looked at it doubtfully. "That Soo — whatever you called it . . . If it eats goat, it must be a meat eater, right?"

"Sootee Lan. Yes, it's a meat eater. It loves goat. We give it the carcasses of goats that have died of old age. It's all right;

we're good friends with the Sootee Lan. It's already agreed to take us, so hop on!"

Balsa sighed and looked at Kassa. "Now I understand. We'll travel the underground waterways. It will certainly be faster, but we might have preferred to walk, don't you think?"

"Mmm." Kassa nodded.

"You go first and I'll sit at the back."

Kassa clambered nervously on behind Yoyo, then Balsa crouched down and slipped gingerly behind him. The creature's skin was much drier than she had expected but it was extremely hard. To her surprise, it was also slightly warm. The water flowing past their lower legs was so cold it cut like a knife. Now she understood why Yoyo had made them rub their legs with *yukkal* juice.

"Hold your spear in your left hand and grip my clothes tightly with your right," Yoyo said. Kassa grabbed his shirt tightly in his fist while Balsa took hold of Kassa's cloak.

"Are — are you sure we'll be all right, Yoyo? You said we'd die if we fell in."

"We'll be fine, Kassa. Just grip tightly with your legs. Sootee Lan won't try to buck you off or anything like that."

"He won't dive underwater, will he?" Balsa asked.

"What? Are you afraid too? Don't worry — you're with me! And off we go!" Yoyo whistled and Sootee Lan began gliding through the water.

The capital of Kanbal spread out across a bowl-shaped valley, nestled in the heart of the Yusa mountains. Encircled by a large outer wall, it was like a giant version of the clan village. The King's Road stretched from the main gate in the south straight through the city to the castle perched on top of a high hill deep inside. A heavy snow had fallen and the white against the damp, black stone of the walls created a strange beauty.

The castle soared above the city, its sturdy walls rooted in solid bedrock. The numerous steeply roofed halls within were joined by covered corridors and topped by tall spires that split the air like spears. The city housed a force of a thousand soldiers from the king's clan, as well as another thousand soldiers taken from each of the other nine clans and changed every ten years. At the moment, an elite troop of five hundred men had gathered within the castle walls. Their leather tents were pitched in the courtyard and smoke from their cooking fires hung thickly in the air. Clearly, they were preparing for war.

King Radalle looked down into the courtyard from the meeting room at the top of a tower. His young face was pale and nervous. "It looks like we're almost ready," he said. He turned around to look at Yuguro, who was standing with his fingertips resting lightly on the huge meeting table. "The troops seem much calmer than I expected. That's a relief. Once the priests perform the rites of power, we can go." He brushed his fine brown hair back from his forehead and looked anxiously around the meeting room, checking to make sure that no one was there. "Are you sure it will be all right?" he whispered to Yuguro. Fear flickered in his eyes. "They say that the Darkness reads the hearts of men. If the *hyohlu* sense that we're plotting against the Mountain King, they'll attack."

Yuguro sighed inwardly, but outwardly he smiled. "Of course it will be all right. We've already gone over this many times. The *hyohlu* won't enter the chamber until I've announced that I've been chosen as the Dancer and the Darkness falls. While the *hyohlu* and I dance, all you need to do is repeat hymns of praise to the Mountain King in your mind. It will all be over in no time. The Last Door will open and your soldiers will pour in to protect you. No matter what happens, you won't be in any danger."

In fact, Yuguro was not in the least worried about the king. Radalle was a weak man; indeed, it was hard to believe that he was really Rogsam's son. As soon as the *hyohlu* appeared, he would be so frightened that he would have no time to think or do anything but pray fervently that he be spared. *The kings of Kanbal have never been more than figureheads. They're just a symbol to unite the clans*, Yuguro reminded himself. *It makes no difference if the king is a coward: It's the Dancer's mettle that will be tested.*

"But . . ." The king looked at him with pleading eyes. "Will you be all right? It's not that I don't believe in your skill. But I can't help but wonder — can you really prevent the *hyohlu* from reading your mind when you dance together?"

Yuguro rapped the table with his knuckles. "We've gone over this time and again. As you know, my elder brother Jiguro was also chosen for the Spear Dance. Before we fought that last time, he gave me his gold ring and taught me everything he knew."

Yuguro's eyes never wavered from the king's. He knew very well that it was best to look people straight in the eye when lying, and the closer a lie was to the truth, the more true it sounded. He had realized when he was young that everyone had something they wanted to believe. If you told them what they wanted to hear, even if it was a lie, they would fall for it easily. The king was afraid, so he wanted someone to reassure him that he would not fail.

"Your Majesty, the Spear Dance is the art of transcending oneself. The mind becomes as clear as water and the body moves of its own accord, as it has been drilled to do. Once I face the *hyohlu*, any enmity I might feel won't matter, because one can't cross spears with another unless one seeks to defeat him. The *hyohlu* will only be watching to see if I can reach a state of true nothingness and perform the dance well."

Yuguro felt almost no anxiety. He was confident that his skill was equal to the Spear Dance, and when his brother had taught him the dance on that overgrown riverbank in the mountains, there really had been no time to think. *Besides, everyone has some evil in his heart*, he reassured himself.

He could not believe that all those who had met the *hyohlu* before had harbored no trace of fear, hate, or desire for *luisha*. Yet there had never been a ceremony in which they had not received the precious gem.

I don't care how many cowards the hyohlu *kill*, he thought. *As long as I succeed in the Spear Dance, the rest will fall into place.* The Yonsa Elder, Laloog, had told him what the *hyohlu* were. The information had made him shudder, and that was precisely why he had decided that none of the others should be told. If the warriors knew the true nature of the *hyohlu*, or why they could read the minds of men, some would be sure to waver in their resolution. That was what Yuguro feared.

He laughed to himself, thinking of those he might face. *I deceived you once before and I'll deceive you again. I'll put you to rest once and for all. Open the door to me, and vanish into the bottom of the Darkness.*

He moved closer to the king. "Your Majesty, your father, King Rogsam, commanded me to protect you. Therefore I must warn you never to show this kind of doubt until the ceremony is over." He held the king's gaze and said in a low voice, "The *hyohlu* who live in the Mountain Deep are not the only ones who can read the minds of men. This world is full of such enemies. The instant they sense any weakness in you, they'll rip out your throat. King Rogsam knew that well."

He allowed his voice to soften into a more coaxing tone. "But of course, this doesn't mean that men never feel any fear. My lord, if ever you are afraid, look to me. I will stand by your side to the end. I am your Spear."

The king blinked and nodded. Yuguro was not lying. He had protected and trained the king for the last ten years, since Radalle ascended the throne at the age of fifteen. And, just as Yuguro had intended, the king remained a puppet in his hands. King Rogsam had been rotten to the core, but his ability to see what was coming and utilize it to his advantage was brilliant. Radalle was his only son, born late into his marriage, and he had doted on him. Yet he had no illusions: Radalle was weak-willed, and, without support, he would be ousted from the throne by Rogsam's brothers. When Rogsam realized that he was dying, he immediately took steps to ensure Radalle's reign.

Rogsam summoned Yuguro to the throne room, where they met alone. Yuguro remembered every moment of that meeting. Eight gold rings and a dagger rested on the table in front of the king, and with a laugh, he had given Yuguro a choice — to become a hero or to be slain on the spot as a rebel. He could, he claimed, create as many reasons to brand Yuguro a traitor as there were stars in the sky; and to underscore the point, he casually described the plot by which he himself had become king. He knew only too well that there was nothing Yuguro could do about it now, even if he wanted to; he would never be able to prove Jiguro's innocence.

Thus he laid out his proposal. Yuguro would travel to New Yogo, find Jiguro, and wrest the spear ring from him.

He would return to Kanbal a hero, bearing all nine rings, and assume the role of Radalle's chief Spear. Then Rogsam's line would live on in the kings of Kanbal, and Yuguro would achieve all the prominence for which he'd hoped.

To Yuguro, Rogsam's proposal was like a dream come true. He felt no compunction whatsoever about deceiving his brother or becoming a hero by falsely claiming he had killed him. Thanks to Jiguro, he had spent much of his life hiding in the shadows, trying to avoid the contempt of the court. To use him as a stepping-stone into the light was a fitting revenge. Rogsam's and Yuguro's interests were thus perfectly aligned.

Again, the fact that Radalle was so easily manipulated and timid proved fortunate for Rogsam. If he had been strong-willed, at some point he and Yuguro must inevitably have clashed, and then Yuguro might have allied himself with a different, more manageable prince. But Radalle would likely live out his days resting comfortably in the palm of Yuguro's hand, and die without questioning the machinations that held him there. Rogsam was sure Yuguro would protect his son in order to maintain his own position as a hero. What better plot than this?

But even Rogsam failed to foresee that Yuguro's ambitions would far exceed what he imagined. While Jiguro was teaching him the Spear Dance, Yuguro had a sudden revelation: None of those who had experienced the last Giving Ceremony would be the right age to participate in the next one. He had hurried back to Kanbal, his heart dancing with a new vision that expanded in front of him — a vast and untouched plain just waiting for his hand to change it. All the young heroes who had shone as Spears by preserving the ancient traditions were dead. If he could consolidate his power and win the trust of the young warriors before the next ceremony, he should be able to develop enough military might to overthrow the Mountain King. Those who were too steeped in tradition to change, who stood in awe of the Mountain King, would by that time be too old to interfere. If he could gain free access to *luisha*, fulfilling the dream of every Kanbalese, his name would never be forgotten. This was the road by which he would become a true hero.

He smiled at the young king. "Tomorrow we'll set out to create a new history for Kanbal."

Sootee Lan glided swiftly and effortlessly along the underground waterway. Kassa feared he would fall off at first, but he soon relaxed and then stared around him in wonder. What surprised him most was the fact that the caves were teeming with life. At first glance the ice-cold water appeared empty, but many fish and water insects swam within it, their transparent bodies glittering. Countless holes dotted the *lyokuhaku* and *hakuma* walls, and here and there Kassa caught glimpses of movement inside. A beautiful, flutelike sound echoed off the stone and down the branch tunnels, creating a complex melody before fading away again.

At first Kassa was so absorbed in this strange new underground world that he had no time to feel bored, but as time passed, he became increasingly uncomfortable. The worst thing was not being able to see the light of day. Although *togal* gave him the ability to see, he desperately missed the gentle touch of sunlight soaking into his body.

At noon on the first day, Yoyo left them in the care of another Herder, who was waiting for them on a rock ledge in Yonsa territory. Kassa felt somewhat forlorn when Yoyo disappeared from sight, as though his last connection to the Musa land had dissolved with his friend. Their new guide was darkly tanned and looked to be in his late thirties. He grinned when he saw Balsa.

"I suppose you don't remember me, do you?" he said. "We used to play together."

"Really?" Balsa stared intently at his small face.

He laughed and shook his head. "Well, I'm not surprised. You were only five at the time. But I remember you very well. You were quite a handful! When I showed you a goat, you insisted on riding it and wouldn't take no for an answer. I let you try, just as a joke, but you actually rode it surprisingly well."

Balsa, embarrassed, rubbed the back of her neck. "Really? Did I do that?"

"You sure did. I was very sad when I heard that you'd died, and very surprised when I got Toto the Elder's message. They had to repeat it for me twice! When I knew you really were alive, well, I just had to meet you again, so I volunteered for this job."

Kassa was grinning, and Balsa laughed and shrugged.

As they rode Sootee Lan smoothly through the dark caves, the Herder, whose name was Nono, continued to regale Balsa with detailed stories of things she barely remembered. It was odd to think that someone still recalled the time when she had been Karuna's daughter. To relieve the monotony and fatigue of the journey, she responded to his questions about her life after she fled with Jiguro. The memories came flooding back with remarkable clarity: the hard days of hiding; the pleasures of her friendships with Tanda and Torogai; her work as an itinerant bodyguard. She told them about her adventures with Chagum, the Guardian of the Spirit, and Nono and Kassa listened as if it were some ancient and fascinating legend. But at one point, Nono interrupted her.

"Nayugu?" he murmured. "You said it's another world, usually invisible to us, but laid over and linked with this one? That sounds like Noyook."

"Noyook?"

"Yes. We too know of this other world. And we call it Noyook." He twisted his head to look back at Balsa. "If you see the door open in the Mountain Deep, you'll get a glimpse of it. The palace of the Mountain King is usually invisible, because it's in Noyook."

Balsa smiled wryly. Nono looked puzzled. "What?" he asked.

"Nothing. It's just that up until now, in my work as a bodyguard, I've mostly dealt with problems like fighting between rich merchants. But lately, I keep running into this mysterious world! It's strange stuff for someone who knows nothing about magic weaving."

The familiar, carefree face of her friend Tanda came to her mind. He would love to take a trip like this, as he always longed to learn more about the strange and extraordinary. Balsa was not really interested in an invisible world regardless of what it was called, but Tanda would be thrilled if she told him that in Kanbal it was called Noyook.

To Balsa, deep under the rock of the mother range, Tanda's hut in the forested mountains of New Yogo seemed very far away. Since the day she and Jiguro had first found their way there when she was ten, they had always returned to that house, no matter where they traveled. It was the closest thing to home that she knew. She pictured the slant-ing rays of the sun falling across the hearth. *Will I ever sit by that fire again and share some stew with Tanda?* When she thought about what lay ahead of her, this did not seem possible.

If I die at the ceremony . . . He would probably still wait for her by that same hearth, without ever knowing what had happened to her.

She took a deep breath and shook her head. *It can't be helped. Magic weavers can see spirits, right, Tanda? If I die, I'll come back to you as a spirit.*

Soon, four days had passed since their departure from Musa territory. The Herder People had been careful to stop when it was night in the outside world so Balsa and Kassa could keep to their sleeping patterns. Their guides from each clan were very kind, but still Kassa and Balsa talked less and less as they drew closer to the ceremony chamber.

On the night of the fourth day, two Herders from the king's territory met them when they stopped. One was quite old and the other young. "From here, we'll walk," they said. Balsa and Kassa thanked Sootee Lan and bid him farewell.

Before they had gone far, they came to a cave shaped like a small plaza. Unlike the other caves they had been through, there was no sign of life, and the space was filled with silence. While she sensed no living creatures, Balsa was overcome by a strange sensation. It seemed as if the very air was watching them.

The Herders stopped, and the older one pointed to a window-sized hole on the far side of the cave. "That hole leads to the ceremony chamber. Go and take a look."

They did as they were told, placing both hands on the edge to peer inside. Just a few steps lower down, they saw a bright space enveloped in a hazy, pearly light.

"Tomorrow at dawn, the king, his Spears, and their attendants will descend into the ceremony chamber."

"What's that light?" Kassa asked.

"The walls of the chamber are alive," the old man said in a hushed voice. "When the day of the ceremony draws near, it begins to glow like this. By that light, the King's Spears compete with each other. When the chosen one summons the *hyohlu*, the light will vanish and complete Darkness will fall."

He looked at Balsa. "You're Jiguro's foster child, I hear."

"Yes."

"Thirty-five years ago, I watched from this hole as Jiguro fought. He was unparalleled."

Balsa nodded. He shifted his eyes to Kassa. "Do you have the letter from Laloog Yonsa?"

Kassa pulled a goatskin scroll from inside his shirt. The string tying it was sealed with wax that bore Laloog's seal.

"Good. Listen then. You'll have only one chance to show that scroll. If you reveal yourself before the spear fight begins, the king will think you're interfering, his men will attack you, and you'll have no chance to escape. But if you wait until after the chosen one summons the *hyohlu*, you'll be in pitch darkness and unable to read the letter.

"The only chance you have to address the warriors and the king is after the chosen one announces himself, but before he summons the *hyohlu* — a very brief moment in time. Once the Dancer is chosen, all the other warriors must place their spears on the ground. If you speak at that moment, you'll still have a chance to escape, no matter what happens afterward. Even if the men plan to storm the Mountain King's palace, they must obey the rules of the ceremony until the *hyohlu* opens the Last Door. Do you understand what you must do?"

Trembling, Kassa clutched the scroll and nodded. The old man smiled for the first time. "Good. You will sleep here tonight. Even if you can't sleep, it will help just to close your eyes and rest. We'll make sure to wake you up before the king and his men arrive."

Setting down a bag of dried grasses and goatskins that he had been carrying, the young Herder quickly made up their beds. Kassa crawled inside but could not sleep. The words he must call out to the warriors kept spinning through his mind, keeping him awake. There seemed to be a cold board in his stomach, and light flashed behind his eyelids at every little sound.

He tossed and turned until Balsa laid her warm hand gently on his shoulder. Slowly and quietly she rubbed his back, and he felt himself relax a little.

The silence underground seeped inside him, and before he knew it, he was asleep.

CHAPTER III
THE CEREMONY BEGINS

At daybreak, a strange sound flowed out of the cave behind the castle and climbed high into the sky. The people called it the Mountain King's Flute. It signaled that the time for the ceremony had come.

Five hundred soldiers were already assembled in front of the cave, standing in files and bearing spears and torches. The king of Kanbal, robed in ceremonial white, passed down the center, between the rows of men. After him came his Spears and their attendants, each with their clan crest embroidered on their chests.

The cave was a huge, gaping fissure where the thunder god, Yoram, was said to have split the towering crag with his bare hand. It was snowing thick and fast, and the sky was dim, despite the dawn. In the snow, the priests quietly performed the rites that would transfer the power of the thunder god to the king and his Spears.

Kahm, breathing white clouds of steam, watched his uncle Yuguro's powerful, hawklike profile. He could discern no trace of either nervousness or excitement. In this world of gray and white, with the flickering flames of the torches dimmed by the powdery snow, everything seemed dreamlike, unreal. Only the dark mouth of the cave stood out starkly against the looming shadow of the cliff.

Yuguro felt the power of the five hundred men behind him. When they poured into the Mountain Deep, he expected that most of them would die. The royal family might curse him for squandering Kanbal's best fighting men, but they could not stop him. He controlled the clan armies down to the last man, for he himself had mentored and trained the elite warriors who led them. Although the king's kin resented Yuguro's influence, even they recognized his superior might. Confidence exuded from his tall, imposing figure, and he seemed to shine like the gold ring on his spear. Dazzled by his radiance, the men would follow him into the depths of the earth. As Yuguro watched the waving hand of the priest, he spared no sympathy for the men behind him, breathing white gusts into the air and fearing death. Instead, he imagined the roar of the masses greeting his victorious return.

When the rites were completed, Yuguro motioned the young Spears to form a circle. "Oh Spears!" he announced in

a firm, ringing tone. "Mightiest warriors of Kanbal! The time
has come for you to use your power to bring wealth to your
poor motherland. Do not forget that when Darkness falls on
the chamber, you must concentrate all your efforts on chant-
ing the praises of the Mountain King. Make sure your
thoughts are sincere. Do you understand?"

The young men nodded, their faces tense. They knew
that death awaited them should they fail.

Yuguro looked at the pale face of his nephew Kahm —
Kahm, who had feared that Yuguro would replace him with
his son, Shisheem. *What a fool*, he thought. He was so like
Jiguro, incapable of being anything but straight and honest,
blind to the fact that Yuguro was making him bear a risk to
which he would never expose his own son.

He turned his eyes away and took a deep breath. "It is
time!" he shouted. "Yoram, god of thunder, may your light
protect us! May our spears strike like lightning!" He raised
his gold spear ring, and the other Spears raised theirs to
touch his.

Kassa and Balsa crouched inside the hole and gazed down
into the chamber, which was gradually growing brighter. The
silence seemed to press painfully against Kassa's ears and his
heart beat loudly in his chest. Then came a sound like the
whistles of the Herder People, echoing repeatedly, overlapping and resounding in a complex melody.

The caves are playing the pipes, Kassa thought. He

understood that the tunnels were like reeds, and the air flowed through them to produce an exquisite music — the Mountain King's Flute.

When it faded, the silence returned. They waited a long time in that silence. Then they heard boots ringing against the stone, and figures emerged into the chamber before their eyes.

They're here.

Long, wavering shadows formed a circle. When they stopped moving, a thin, shrill voice, shaking pitifully with nervousness, proclaimed, "O, Mountain King! I, King of Kanbal, the land on which the sun shines, have come! Accom — accompanied by my Spears! We have come to demonstrate our mastery of the spear and the sincerity of our hearts."

As soon as his voice stopped echoing off the walls, the shadowy figures in the room began to move. With a shout, all the men spun to face their partners, and the air rang with the clash of colliding spear shafts. Balsa and Kassa leaned forward to watch the combatants from their hiding place. In the faint light, a young attendant with a boyish face confronted a Spear in his prime, their spears striking fiercely. Although the youth moved with admirable skill and speed, in the end he was no match for the seasoned warrior.

Kahm came into view next. He threw his heart and soul into the match and defeated the first Spear, but the second knocked his weapon to the ground. Watching them, Balsa realized what an extraordinary feat it had been for Jiguro to become the Dancer at only sixteen years of age.

Finally Yuguro stepped into their range of vision. When Balsa saw him whirl his spear and snap it into position, she caught her breath sharply. Each clan had its own moves, and watching Yuguro was like watching Jiguro. Although all the Spears were impressive spear-wielders, he was by far the best.

Kassa felt his heart constrict in his chest as he watched each match reach its conclusion. The skin across his forehead felt numb and he was drenched in a cold sweat.

Not yet.

He saw Yuguro twist his final opponent's spear up into the air and out of his grasp.

Not yet.

Yuguro rapped the butt end of his spear sharply on the floor. At this signal, all the other warriors laid their spears on the ground. In a clear, resonant voice to which King Radalle's could never compare, he declared, "I, Yuguro Musa, am the greatest spearman of them all!"

At that moment, Balsa gave Kassa a light shove on the shoulder. He felt himself sliding down through the hole. The noise of his feet hitting the floor shattered the silence. The men, whose eyes had been focused on Yuguro in the center of the circle, turned toward him in shock.

"Kassa?" he heard Kahm whisper in surprise.

Kassa took a deep breath, lifted high the scroll he gripped in his hand, and shouted, "I, Kassa, son of Tonno of the

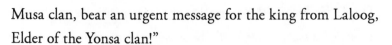

Musa clan, bear an urgent message for the king from Laloog, Elder of the Yonsa clan!"

No one moved. The men stared thunderstruck, unable to comprehend what was happening.

Kassa's eyes searched the room until he caught sight of a young man, crowned and wearing white — the king. He started toward him.

"Hold!" Kassa saw Yuguro swing his spear toward him and froze. "What trap is this? Are you some monster that lives in the Deep?"

"No! Uncle Yuguro, it's me!" Kassa yelled frantically. "Laloog the Elder, who was here at the last ceremony, entrusted me with a message to save your lives. Your Majesty! King's Spears! Attendants! You are misled! If you go ahead with this plan, Kanbal will be destroyed. Your Majesty, please read the Elder's message!"

Yuguro lunged at Kassa with his spear, and Kassa took a step back in fear. But before his uncle could reach him, Yuguro was seized from behind. "What's the meaning of this?" he shouted, twisting his head to see who held him. "Kahm, is that you? Are you mad? Release me!"

But Kahm held him fast and did not let go. "Uncle, what are you doing? Were you going to kill Kassa?"

"You fool! Don't be taken in! That's not Kassa! It's some creature in his guise. It's testing us!"

"And if you're wrong?" Kahm shouted back. "If he really does have a message from Laloog, what will you do then?

The Elder knows the secrets of the Mountain Deep. Maybe he sent Kassa to warn us about something we don't know before it's too late."

The warriors muttered in confusion. Kassa turned to the king. "Your Majesty! Read this message and decide for yourself who is right — Uncle Yuguro or me."

Yuguro twisted around to look at the king. "Your Majesty, don't be deceived. This is a trap to make us lose courage!"

The king looked from Kassa to Yuguro, bewildered. Seeing the panic in his face, Kassa pleaded, "Your Majesty. If you don't read this message, you will most certainly die here. It was written to save you. Please believe me!"

"Your Majesty! Remember our great dream!" Yuguro roared. The king looked at him, imploring, and Yuguro gazed back steadily. "You must believe *me*, Yuguro, who has always shielded you from danger."

The king exhaled noisily, his lips trembling. It looked like he was about to nod his assent.

"No!" Kassa screamed. "Your Majesty! If you don't read this message, the *hyohlu* will kill you! And not just you — they'll kill everyone here!"

The king started and looked at him. Close to tears, Kassa pleaded again. "Your Majesty, please, don't let them die. Don't destroy Kanbal!"

Yuguro looked around at the Spears and said, in a commanding tone, "Someone capture him! Have you forgotten our mission? Remember why you're here!"

Several men moved forward hesitantly. *It's no use,* Kassa thought despairingly. Yuguro had a firm grasp on their hearts and minds. The king in particular seemed to depend on him like a little child. No matter how Kassa might try to convince him, in the end, he would do as Yuguro said.

So Kassa did the only thing he could. Leaping back to the wall, he ripped off the string that bound the scroll. Shaking it open, he held it high and began to read:

"I, Laloog, participant in the ceremony of the Mountain Deep, convey to you its secret. I pray that my words may reach you before you summon the hyohlu, *Guardians of the Darkness."*

The Spears who had started toward him stopped, hesitating.

"The Guardians of the Darkness are not servants of the Mountain King. They are those who have left this world, your —"

Kahm, distracted by Kassa, suddenly felt Yuguro drop from his grasp, and the next instant he was flying through the air. He barely managed to roll into a defensive ball before he slammed into the rock floor. The force knocked the breath out of him, and he lay still, dazed and winded. Yuguro lunged toward Kassa with his spear. Unable to dodge, Kassa stood mesmerized as the point plunged toward his stomach. Just before it pierced his flesh, however, it veered aside with a sharp clang and a trail of white light. Kassa fell to the ground as someone shoved him roughly aside. Yuguro's spear flew from his hands and clattered to the cave floor. It all happened so fast that he could only stare blankly at the figure whose spear now pointed directly at his throat.

"You!" he gasped.

"It's been a long time, Master Yuguro," Balsa said. "The last time we met was three years before Jiguro died, wasn't it?" Yuguro paled. "I hear you claim to have killed him and taken back the spear rings." She smiled bitterly. "You lie! Jiguro died of an illness. I was by his side the whole time."

She looked at the king, who was cowering by the wall, his face rigid with fear. "Your Majesty, I am Balsa Yonsa, daughter of Karuna, physician to your uncle, King Naguru. Your father, King Rogsam, sent his assassins to murder my father and make it look like a robbery. I too would have been killed but for Jiguro Musa, who rescued me. He saved my life."

The murmuring of the crowd grew louder, but Yuguro kept his eyes on Balsa. She had only thrown him off balance for a moment. He said loudly, "You fool! Did you think that you could trick us like this?"

Balsa frowned, wondering what he meant. He continued calmly, "First Kassa, and now Jiguro's foster child! I know many illusions appear in the Mountain Deep to test those who enter, but listen carefully, servant of the Mountain King! I have been chosen as the Dancer. None of the King's Spears are foolish enough to be swayed by you, no matter what you might say." He turned to the Spears. "Isn't that right? You, the King's Spears, the greatest warriors in

Kanbal — you'll stand with me no matter what." He saw the hesitation in their faces. "I would stand with you," he said quietly. Then he turned to Balsa and spread out both hands. "So, you monster of the Deep! If you have been sent to kill me, do so, if that is truly the wish of the Mountain King."

Balsa stared in amazement at the man who stood before her with his arms spread wide. *He is the real monster,* she thought. *He feels no shame at all that he betrayed Jiguro, his own brother, to become a false hero.* She remembered Jiguro's joy and relief when he had passed on the Spear Dance and the gold ring, and a wave of nausea rose from deep in her chest. This worthless man had taken all the misery they had endured and exploited it to his own advantage: Jiguro's agony at having to slay his own friends, his grief-stricken face streaming with tears, the days of hunger and sleeping in the mud, the shudder of his spear in his hands as he plunged it into flesh — just to make enough money for them to survive. The rage that had simmered and smoldered inside her since she was a child flared into a white-hot flame.

Softly she lowered the point of her spear to the ground and slipped it under Yuguro's spear, flipping it toward him. She gazed at him with a cold smile on her lips. "I'm impressed. It appears I have no hope of defeating you in a war of words. If you insist that I am a dweller of the Deep, then so be it — I will play your game. But only the strongest spear-wielder is chosen for the Dance, yes?" She swung her spear once through the air and leveled it. "Come, then, and see what the spear of Jiguro can do."

In a thunderous voice, she shouted, "Yuguro of the Musa clan! I, Balsa of the Yonsa clan, raised by Jiguro, challenge you! Guardians of the Darkness, watch carefully, and judge who truly deserves to join the Dance."

As soon as the words had left her mouth, the light in the chamber dimmed. Balsa and the warriors looked up, startled. Behind them stood shadows deeper than their own.

CHAPTER IV
DANCE OF VENGEANCE

Stillness filled the chamber. They felt as if the Darkness itself were watching them.

"It looks like they answered," Balsa commented.

Yuguro's mouth lifted in a smile. "So it does. Fine. I accept your challenge. Come!"

In his heart, he was laughing. *What arrogance! She thinks a mere woman can beat me! That's like baring her throat and asking me to kill her.* Then a white flash grazed the side of his neck and he shrank back in surprise. Before he could register the searing pain, a blur of lights seemed to shoot toward his throat and he leapt away.

An icy chill swept through him. Never before had he encountered a spear that moved so swiftly and with such deadly accuracy. He opened his eyes wide and exhaled sharply. Any trace of contempt had vanished. All that remained was a burning hate. He took a deep breath, and energy radiated from him, electrifying the very air.

In a streak of light, his spear tip blazed toward Balsa's face, and she swiftly leaned away from it. The spear point vanished, only to leap up at her from below. Reflexively, she knocked it aside with her spear grip, swinging her own weapon around to strike his knees. He jumped and brought his spear down upon her from above. Balsa repelled the stroke, but the force of the impact made her hands tingle. A chill raced up her neck as Yuguro's spear point snaked toward her — from the right, then left, then from below. She parried each blow, slowly pressing forward. They were almost evenly matched. Kahm had finally regained consciousness, and he stood motionless with the other warriors and Kassa, watching spellbound as the two spears collided like bolts of lightning.

Then the spears crossed, each fighter aiming at the other's throat. Blood spurted from Yuguro's chin and Balsa's cheek. Yuguro turned his face aside at the blow, but Balsa did not, and that difference tipped the balance. She thrust her spear through Yuguro's shoulder, then pulled it out, kicking him in the chest as she withdrew. He fell writhing to the ground.

Rage consumed Balsa as she approached him, the blood pounding in her temples. She gazed down at him where he lay moaning, one hand pressed against his shoulder, and she murmured, "Now you die." Raising her spear, she brought it down with all her might —

And in that instant, all light disappeared and the world plunged into darkness.

Balsa felt the blow she had aimed at Yuguro repelled and leapt back. Then she froze. In the pitch darkness, she sensed rather than saw a hazy blue figure standing between her and the prostrate Yuguro, looking down at him. She felt the hair rise on the nape of her neck, and goose bumps covered her skin.

The shape of that blue shadow seemed impossibly familiar. *It can't be . . .* The words of Laloog's message floated into her mind. *"The Guardians of the Darkness are not servants of the Mountain King. They are those who have left this world, your —"*

It can't be.

She peered at the shadows in the darkness that surrounded the ring of warriors. She recognized one of them, and then another and another.

It can't be.

An icy coldness washed over Yuguro and set his teeth chattering as he stared up at the blue figure. The cold was so intense it numbed the burning pain in his shoulder.

What's this? Am I dreaming?

He tried to scramble backward. Those eyes watching him from the darkness — they belonged to a man he knew well. *You mean you're still alive?* But the energy radiating from the shadow above him was not that of living flesh and blood.

Through the pain and fear that gripped him, he suddenly remembered what Laloog had told him. *Of course. I forgot. You're a* hyohlu. *And I've come to put you out of your misery, to send you back to the bottom of Darkness.* Desperately he searched for the right words to convince it to return to the land of the dead. "Brother," he whispered, "do you blame me? Perhaps what I did seems unfair. But surely you can understand. I had no choice. It was the only way to redeem the honor of the Musa clan.

"It must have been hard for you, brother. Very hard. But I'll ease your suffering; I'll ease your pain. Open the door to the palace of the Mountain King — for the sake of the people of Kanbal, for their happiness. You understand, don't you? This is the only way I can save you. . . .

"If you do this, Kanbal will become a rich nation. No one will go hungry, you see? Your people will be filled with gratitude. The shame you bore will become a tragic legend, and your life will at last have meaning!"

Yuguro looked up at the figure expectantly. But it did not respond. It merely gazed at him silently with those dark eyes, apparently unmoved by his words.

As Yuguro gazed back, anger and disgust slowly welled inside him. *You fool!* he thought. *You pitiful man, clinging to past tragedy just because the path you chose ended in disaster. Yet you dare to blame me! You terrible, terrible fool!*

Something inside him snapped with twenty-five years of suppressed anger. *Damn you! It's me who should blame you!*

Do you realize what you did to my life by fleeing Kanbal for someone else's daughter? Do you know how I felt all those years I spent trying to be invisible? How I hated you!

A burning rage filled his chest and his hand moved of its own accord. He felt it reach behind his back to unsheath his dagger. He knew that he should stop himself, but the desire to cut this man down was overpowering. He swung the dagger out sideways and stabbed the shadow in the leg.

Instantly, a fiery pain shot up his own leg. He screamed. The smell of blood filled the darkness and blood spurted from the wound with every heartbeat. *What happened? Why am I hurt?* Gasping for breath, he backed away. In his terror, he could no longer think clearly. *Die, damn you! You're dead already! How long are you going to keep ruining my life? If you'd just go away, the glory would be mine!* Sobbing, he groped for his spear in the darkness and pulled it toward him. He felt the shadow stoop over him, reading his thoughts. In his heart, he shrieked, *If you're truly my brother, give me the lui-sha! Make up for what you did to me! Give it to me!*

And then die already! Go back into the darkness forever!

He felt nothing but hate for the one who stood there.

Balsa felt a deep sadness surge through the darkness. The familiarity of it struck her with such painful intensity that she staggered. Each time Jiguro had killed one of his friends, she had been there watching, never averting her eyes. And she had felt what he felt, as if the emotion bled from his back and shoulders — a sorrow so sharp and tangible she could almost touch it. . . .

That same grief now flooded from the *hyohlu* that bent over Yuguro.

He's going to kill him. . . . And it makes him sad. . . .

Yuguro drew his spear back and then drove it at his opponent with all his might. Like a mirror image, the *hyohlu* raised his spear and struck. But just before its point rammed home, Balsa blocked it with her spear and swung it up in a wide arc away from Yuguro.

The *hyohlu* leveled his spear at her. In that instant, all doubt was banished from her mind. They had crossed spears thousands of times for sixteen years and more.

Jiguro. A hot lump rose in her throat. *You mustn't kill Yuguro. If you do, you'll grieve forever.*

In the same way she had felt his sorrow, anger now seeped from his shadow. Suddenly his spear flashed toward her, slicing through the darkness. Startled, she parried the blow and turned it aside. He struck again, and she parried again. With each exchange, they moved away from Yuguro to face each other alone. Their spears struck with blinding speed until, gradually, their movements melded into a fluid, rhythmical dance.

"The Spear Dance has begun," the old Herder whispered in Kassa's ear. Although it was pitch dark, the Dancers' thoughts and feelings hummed and flashed in the heart of

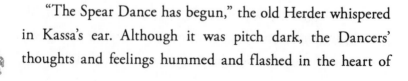

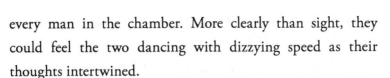

every man in the chamber. More clearly than sight, they could feel the two dancing with dizzying speed as their thoughts intertwined.

"Pray for them, Kassa," the Herder whispered. "Pray that Balsa will be able to lay the *hyohlu* to rest."

As they danced, each thrust and jab of Jiguro's spear seemed to transmit his emotions. One violent thrust grazed her side, and she felt his pent-up hatred burning in the open wound. He hated her! This realization shocked her, yet somewhere deep inside she had always known.

If only I hadn't had to care for you . . .

How many times he must have suppressed that thought. If he had not sworn to care for her, he never would have been forced to kill his friends. If he had not been burdened with her life, he never would have had to flee Kanbal. Rogsam was not the only one who had derailed his life; Balsa had too. Jiguro attacked relentlessly, and each time he broke through her guard, agony ripped through her, permeating her very bones. And waves of hate rolled from the eight other *hyohlu* who stood in the darkness, spears in hand. *But for you*, they whispered, *we would not have had to die so young.*

A bone-gnawing pain sank into her chest, and as it did so, something stirred deep inside her — a fierce, aching rage. All the feelings she had locked deep in her heart, hidden even from herself, burst forth unchecked.

Then tell me, what could I have done? she lashed back,

229

repelling Jiguro's spear. *I was only six years old! Are you saying I should never have been born? Or that I should have killed myself?* She drove her spear at him and felt the hard shock in her hands as he blocked the blow.

I never asked you to save me! It was your choice, not mine!

Her spear grazed his arm and she saw him recoil.

Did you think I didn't know? Did you think I didn't feel how you resented me every time you had to kill a friend? I always knew!

Her cries were directed not only at Jiguro but also at the eight *hyohlu* who stood watching.

Your deaths hurt me. They cut me to the core. And the pain they caused could never be relieved because I could never hope to atone for them.

Her spear tip sliced across Jiguro's ribs.

Even after you died, even to this day, I still carry that burden!

His own spear shot toward her, and with a great wordless cry, she turned it aside. It flew up, leaving his chest unguarded. If she drove her spear home, he would die. In the darkness, she felt his eyes on her. She thought she heard his voice.

Kill me then, Balsa, he seemed to say. *Take all your rage and kill me. Then find your way through to the other side.*

At the sound of his voice, a warm, moist sadness welled up inside her, as if large drops of rain had begun to fall, one by one, on the bleak, parched sands of her fury. Her skin recalled the smell and warmth of his body as he held her in his arms at night, when they huddled in the mud beneath the eaves of some shop in the freezing rain.

Despite his grief and pain, at times weeping with the burden, still he had protected her, embraced her, raised her. . . .

She felt him drive his spear toward her, inviting her to attack. Though she knew the blow was aimed directly at her heart, she did not move. It pierced her chest. Pain exploded through her body, and she saw herself die. In the agony of that death, she staggered toward Jiguro and threw her arms around the darkness there.

His warm, familiar presence enveloped her. Her feelings for him and his for her turned to warmth . . . then fused together. She heard him whisper in her heart, *Farewell, Balsa.*

She had been stabbed to the heart, and she could still feel the terrible pain; but nothing flowed from the wound, nor did she smell blood. A soft blue light radiated from her arms where she embraced him, illuminating the chamber, and suddenly, light blazed from the other *hyohlu* as well. She felt Jiguro melt from her arms, vanishing into that blue light. When the warmth of his body faded from hers, only loneliness lingered, like a thin wisp of smoke trailing up from a quenched candlewick.

Kassa, who had been watching in stunned amazement, suddenly realized that the rock floor beneath his feet had become transparent. The king screamed and his Spears

231

cowered in fear, crouching down and hugging themselves at the sight of what lay beneath them.

Then suddenly they were floating in water from the chest down — water infinitely deep and so breathtakingly clear it seemed they were floating in midair. Yet, strangely, it did not feel cold at all. The lights radiated by Jiguro and the other *hyohlu* encircled Balsa and fused together, holding her for one last moment in their warmth. Then the light passed on, flowing away through the water to embrace the others in turn. As the light touched them, each one heard a whispered farewell. The thoughts and feelings of a father, a brother, or an uncle tragically wrenched from this world softly touched their hearts and vanished.

With stunned faces they watched the blue light merge with the water and spread ever outward until it penetrated the rock walls. The gray stone began to change and glow with an unearthly blue light. Suddenly they realized what they were looking at and gasped, thunderstruck.

Luisha! The luminous stone!

The transparent blue light wrapped itself around them. One of the Spears timidly tried to touch the *luisha,* but though his hand seemed to reach it, he felt nothing. Just then, Balsa saw something waver far below, deep beneath the surface of the water. The blue light shimmered as something enormous began swirling slowly upward. . . .

The Sootee Lan? she wondered, but immediately realized that it was far too big — and too clear. Everyone stared with bated breath, watching the creature spiral toward them. It was a huge, transparent water snake. It had no eyes, and even its innards were transparent, so that it seemed to be made of water. But its scales were dazzlingly beautiful; they glittered blue as it ascended, rubbing its body slowly against the rocks.

For each time the water serpent scraped against the wall, the *luisha* rubbed off onto its scales, shimmering; and whenever it swirled and glided through the water, the life-filled water penetrated the surrounding rock. They watched, mesmerized by the serpent's dance. No one moved, not even the terrified king. The gifts of cheese and dried goat meat that had been piled on the floor of the ceremony chamber bobbed in the water, where they too were transformed into shapes of hazy blue light. To Kassa, it seemed that the hopes and dreams of the people who made them had been turned into light — and swallowed by the serpent.

For a second, Balsa thought she glimpsed Jiguro's face reflected in its scales, which shone like mother of pearl. Perhaps it was just an illusion. But rather than the grim and forbidding face Balsa remembered, he looked bright and joyful, much like Kassa. Tears welled in her eyes, and she covered her face with her hands and wept.

The serpent's dance gradually began to change. Its scales shimmered and rippled, and its skin wrinkled each time its body brushed against the rocks. Kassa suddenly realized what was happening: The snake was shedding. Its skin began to loosen gradually, radiating ripples of rainbow light. As it peeled off, the serpent inside seemed to vanish. The body beneath, which lacked any *luisha* coating, was as clear as water.

Once its skin had been shed, a warm and tender affection, like that of a parent for its child, emanated from the creature, embracing the men where they floated in the water and causing them to tremble. Then it turned and began swimming down to the bottom, the water swirling gently, until all that was left was its beautiful skin, shimmering in the water.

Realizing instantly what they must do, Kassa called to the king, who seemed spellbound by the blue light. "Your Majesty!"

The king turned absently. Kassa pointed to the skin. "It's *luisha*! The gift of the Mountain King."

The king blinked and looked at him, then at the huge snakeskin floating on the water. "You mean . . . Am I supposed to go and get it?"

When Kassa nodded, the king looked around desperately for Yuguro. But he was nowhere to be seen. While he hesitated, the luminous blue skin slowly began to sink.

Losing his patience, Kahm roared, "Your Majesty! Do you intend to let the people of Kanbal starve?"

The king looked at him in surprise. Then he took a deep breath and dived under the water. They saw his hands grasp the skin, but it was too big. He could not manage it on his own, though he struggled valiantly, holding it with one hand as he tried to swim to the surface.

The King's Spears and attendants looked at one another and then at Balsa and Kassa. They nodded and, as one, everyone dived down beneath the water. Although they had not consulted beforehand, they automatically spread out in a circle and grabbed the skin. It was much heavier than they expected, and they had to swim with all their might, twisting and squirming until finally their heads burst to the surface.

Suddenly the light dimmed, and they looked around in astonishment. The water had vanished and they were not even wet. They lay on their stomachs on the floor of the ceremony chamber. The snakeskin that they had clutched so tightly had disappeared, and in its place lay a pile of softly glowing *luisha*.

A beautiful and intricate music filled the cave. They raised their heads, surprised. A group of Herder People had entered the cave and surrounded them, their eyes glowing with *togal*. They began to sing a seemingly ancient song in high, melodious voices:

Rejoice! The People of the Mountain King have come to speak to thee!
The old King of the Mountain is dead. A new king is born!
The old Spears have found true death. A new journey of life has begun!
The old King of Kanbal is dead. A new king is born!

Their voices flowed through the labyrinth, clear and resonant.

> *May the luminous stone,* luisha, *worn by the old Mountain*
>   *King, become the bread of the children of Kanbal.*
> *Oh Spears, didst thou see the Darkness in the Mountain*
>   *Deep?*
>   *Didst thou see the Darkness of thy forebears?*
> *When thy bones return to the earth of Kanbal,*
> *Then wilt thou become the* hyohlu, *Guardians of the*
>   *Darkness.*
>   *Become the* hyohlu, *Guardians of the Darkness,*
>   *and guard the life of the mother range*
> *Until the Dancer comes to turn thy Darkness into light.*

Kassa's eyes filled with tears as he listened to the song. Wiping them away with his sleeve, he looked over at Balsa. Their eyes met, and he bowed deeply.

EPILOGUE
BEYOND THE DARKNESS

The cave that led from Musa territory to New Yogo yawned wide in the warm spring sunshine. Multicolored flowers covered the grassy space before it, and birds warbled in the bushes, rejoicing at the advent of spring.

Balsa hitched her bag higher on her back.

"You're really going?" Gina asked.

"Yes," she said firmly. "I've rested long enough."

After the Herders' song had ended, Balsa and Kassa slipped from the chamber unnoticed. Guided once again by the Herder People, they had traveled underground, returning quietly to Musa territory. Toto the Elder, who met them in the caves, was clearly relieved to see them. He looked up at Balsa and murmured, "Forgive me for leaving so many things unsaid when I sent you on that journey."

She gazed back at him steadily. "You knew, didn't you? You knew who waited for me under the earth."

Toto nodded. "When the *hyohlu* dropped the *luisha* for Gina to find, I immediately suspected that they were summoning someone. Then I met you and, as I listened to your tale of Jiguro, I realized that you were the only person who could hope to lay the *hyohlu* to rest. The Spear Dance can only be danced when your soul is completely exposed. The *hyohlu* throws all his emotions at his partner. Their souls become so close that it's impossible to tell whose feelings are whose." He smiled suddenly. "But even so, usually the Spear Dance is not that difficult. The Dancer doesn't need to be an outstanding person. As long as he can connect with the *hyohlu*'s soul and let him unburden himself, *luisha* has always been given.

"This year, however, we were very worried. Not only Jiguro, but so many other *hyohlu* had been betrayed and murdered. Never had we seen *hyohlu* as difficult to lay to rest as these. And that is why I think they must have been waiting for you. Waiting for you to visit Kanbal . . . For who else could possibly have danced the Spear Dance and brought them peace?"

Balsa shrugged. "Are you saying that because they were waiting for me, the ceremony was delayed more than ten years? You're wrong. Because if that were true, if I hadn't decided on a whim to return to Kanbal, the ceremony would never have taken place."

Toto grinned. "You would have come back. Because it was your destiny."

Balsa shook her head. "I'm sorry, but I disagree. Destiny is just a convenient interpretation to help us accept the past. It wasn't me they were waiting for."

"Then who do you think they *were* waiting for?"

"King Radalle."

Toto raised his eyebrows at her reply. "Why do you think that?"

She sighed slightly. "I think that they were waiting for the new king to become old enough after Rogsam's reign ended. Because the *hyohlu* certainly would never have given *luisha* to a king like Rogsam. In the end, thirty-five years passed before the next ceremony could take place. . . . But . . ."

Toto waited silently for her to continue. She hesitated and then said in a low voice, "I think that Jiguro was waiting for me. Because he came all the way out to meet me when I came back. So you're probably right in that respect — that my return was the reason they decided to start the ceremony."

Toto nodded. Then he said cheerfully, "We Herders call *luisha* the 'heart stone.' The *hyohlu* take all the hopes and sorrows from their lives, turn them into blue light, and return them to the earth, so the *hyohlu* can finally die a true death. So the blue light of *luisha* is really all the thoughts and wishes of men. You laid Jiguro to rest and his feelings turned into *luisha,* which will one day become the bread of life that feeds the people of Kanbal."

Balsa sighed again and smiled. "It was so different from what I imagined as a child when I heard stories of the Mountain King's palace made of *luisha,* and the Last Door."

Toto smiled back. "By what name could we possibly call the great Mountain King, who carves the rock beneath the Yusa mountains with his own body? He makes the roads for the water to pass, and thus brings life to all Yusa. Would you call him a god? A spirit?" He shook his head. "Like a brilliantly shining cocoon that protects the life inside it, we use simple words to spin many tales in order to guard our king."

When Toto had led them outside into the sunlight, the snow-covered land had glittered with a brilliance that cheered their hearts. Kassa breathed a lungful of clear, bracing air and felt a deep satisfaction fill his chest along with it.

When Balsa and Kassa returned to the chieftain's hall, Kaguro came to greet them, his expression reflecting his mixed feelings. As he listened to their tale of the events under the mountain, the frown on his face softened, and when they had finished, he thanked Kassa quietly. One of his younger brothers had been freed from the Darkness, while the other had been trapped within. Yet he felt as though a painful ache in his heart was gone.

To the rest of the clan, Kassa was still nothing more than a youth belonging to a branch family. But Kassa returned to that life quite gladly. When spring came and it was time to take the goats up the mountain with the Herder People, he no longer felt discouraged. The Herders accepted him as one of their own and taught him many secrets of the mountains. Besides, what he had seen on his journey on the underground river had shown him the connection between the life force in the Mountain Deep and the abundant springs and rivers that pushed their way through the earth. Now he could see that the work of the Herders and that of the King's Spears were, in essence, one and the same.

Yuguro never returned from under the mountain. Although his body lived in the house of healing deep inside the king's castle, his mind remained always behind in the Darkness. He woke at daybreak and ate what was put before him, and at night he slept. But though his eyes were open, they were empty. Words, which he had once manipulated so skillfully, never passed his lips. Perhaps one day someone would meet his soul in the ceremony chamber. Whether or not he ever found peace would rest in the hands of the Dancer.

Balsa told young King Radalle what his father, Rogsam, had plotted. But she did not ask him to tell his people. She had already told Jiguro's story to everyone who needed to know it, and she saw no point in stirring up trouble or ousting the young king from his throne when there was no outstanding leader to replace him. Although timid, he still retained some purity and innocence, and it made more sense to slip this secret into his heart so that he would ponder its meaning. Having seen the depths of the Darkness, he might just be a better ruler than any of his kin.

The whole country rejoiced at the gift of *luisha*. Those who had shared Yuguro's dream of invading the Mountain Deep relegated it to the past and behaved as if the plan had never been conceived; only a handful of men knew what had really happened under the mountain, and they would keep that knowledge engraved in their hearts forever. Back under the mountain, when the Herders had finished their sacred hymn, they made the warriors vow to keep silent, and the warriors had agreed, knowing that words could never adequately describe what they had just seen or experienced. If they tried to explain the impossible, the truth would be subtly twisted and changed; it was far better to remain silent and to convince the people that there was a mysterious, indescribable Darkness in this world.

The men would never forget what they had felt when the blue light of the *hyohlu* had caressed them. In that instant, they had known without a doubt that the Guardians of the Darkness were the souls of their own fathers, brothers, and uncles who had departed from this world long before. They also saw that the *hyohlu* were not the servants of the Mountain King, but the very conscience of Kanbal. They guarded the Yusa mountains, the mother range that conferred and supported life; and when the warriors who had witnessed the ceremony departed this life, they too would become *hyohlu* and pass on to their descendants the Darkness and the blue light. Knowing that there existed an invisible, intangible world and a spirit who held up the Yusa range, they would become the Last Door protecting that spirit, and thus they would guard the life of Kanbal. That was the vow they made under the mountain, just like the Spears before them.

As for Balsa, she spent the blustery winter days at her aunt Yuka's house of healing, regaining her strength. While the wounds inflicted by Yuguro healed quickly, those made by the *hyohlu* did not. For many days she left her spear out of reach and simply slept. Her body felt leaden, like an empty shell. Her heart, pierced through by Jiguro's spear, ached for a long time, but while she slept, the pain gradually ebbed until it was just a dull twinge. At last, she was able to rise from her bed and sit near the fire, talking with her aunt a little more each day. Yuka listened to Balsa relate the tale of her journey to the Mountain Deep and what had happened in the Darkness. It was like listening to an old folk tale. As they spoke, the chains that had bound Jiguro and Karuna in their hearts gradually loosened and fell away. Someday, they might be able to remember the dead with gladness and not such sharp sorrow.

The season of the deep snows passed, and the warm rays of the sun softened the hard crust of the drifts. One morning, Balsa's room was filled with a familiar fragrance — simmering herbs. Her aunt was making medicine. As soon as she smelled it, Balsa felt a strong longing to see her friend Tanda, the healer. *It must be the height of spring now in the Misty Blue Mountains.* He would be out picking herbs, humming carelessly to himself.

It's time to go home and tell him about my travels. She opened the window wide and felt the moist spring breeze on her face.

Kassa, Gina, Yoyo, and Toto the Elder went with her to the cave to see her off. Toto gave her a bag containing *togal* and *yukkal* leaves, and plenty of good *laga*, just as he had when she and Kassa set off for the Mountain Deep. Gina gave her a bag of *jokom*, a nut-filled cake baked to last for long journeys.

Hesitantly, Kassa held out a copper spear ring to fit on her shaft, just under the point. "Uh, this is my spear ring. I'd, um, like you to have it."

He must have put his heart and soul into polishing it, for it shone like gold. Balsa smiled and took it. Then she removed her own spear ring, blackened with long use and the blood of others. She gripped it in her hand and looked at Kassa.

"It's dirty, but I took this ring from Jiguro's spear shaft. It protected both our lives." She placed it on the palm of her hand and held it out. "Will you accept it?"

Kassa took the ring and slipped it into place on his own spear. Then he looked up at her and smiled shyly. "Both you and Jiguro were chosen as the Dancer. I wonder if I really have what it takes to use it."

Balsa placed a hand on his shoulder. "I can't read the future, but I can tell you this. If your skill with the spear continues to develop, you'll be good enough to become the Dancer. Be a good spearman, Kassa."

His smile slowly transformed into a bright grin.

Balsa raised her hand in farewell and turned abruptly toward the mouth of the cave. On the other side lay the Misty Blue Mountains, filled with the soft light of spring. With her thoughts fixed on those green mountain slopes, she strode boldly into the darkness.

THE
MUSA CLAN

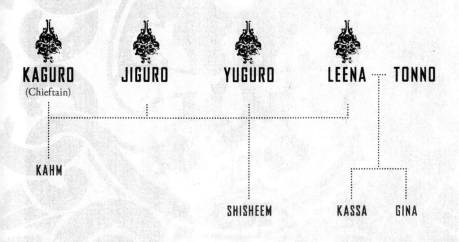

KAGURO
(Chieftain)

JIGURO

YUGURO

LEENA ···· TONNO

KAHM

SHISHEEM

KASSA   GINA

THE
YONSA CLAN

YUKA   KARUNA

BALSA

LIST OF
CHARACTERS

BALSA YONSA an itinerant female bodyguard and skilled spear-wielder; raised by Jiguro

KARUNA YONSA Balsa's father; the physician to Naguru, the former king of Kanbal

JIGURO MUSA Balsa's foster father; a renowned and unparalleled spear-wielder

NAGURU former king of Kanbal; assassinated on the orders of his younger brother, Rogsam

ROGSAM previous king of Kanbal who usurped the throne from his older brother, Naguru

RADALLE Rogsam's son; the current king of Kanbal

MUSA CLAN

KASSA son of Tonno and Leena

GINA Kassa's younger sister

TONNO father of Kassa and Gina; overlord of the Herder People

LEENA mother of Kassa and Gina; younger sister of Kaguro, Jiguro, and Yuguro

KAGURO chieftain of the Musa clan; elder brother of Jiguro, Yuguro, and Leena

YUGURO younger brother of Kaguro and Jiguro; a hero and the most respected of the King's Spears

KAHM eldest son of Kaguro

SHISHEEM eldest son of Yuguro

DOM head of the Musa chieftain's guard; younger brother of Yuguro's wife

YONSA CLAN

YUKA Balsa's aunt and Karuna's younger sister; physician who runs a house of healing

LALOOG former chieftain of the Yonsa clan; an Elder respected by all the clans as witness to the last Giving Ceremony

TAGURU eldest son of Laloog; killed by Jiguro

LUKE younger son of Laloog; current chieftain of the Yonsa tribe

DAHGU grandson of Laloog; one of the King's Spears

HERDER PEOPLE

TOTO known as Toto the Elder; oldest of all the Herders

YOYO a young Herder; Kassa's friend

DODO Yoyo's father

NAHNA Yoyo's mother

NONO childhood friend of Balsa

TANDA a healer and apprentice magic weaver; Balsa's childhood friend

CHAGUM Crown Prince of New Yogo who was once the Guardian of the Spirit

TOROGAI the greatest magic weaver of the time

LIST OF
KANBALESE TERMS

GANLA spicy vegetable

GASHA a type of potato that grows even in poor soil

HAKUMA a translucent white stone

HYOHLU Guardian of the Darkness

JOKOM a nut-filled sweet

KAHL a heavy, woollen, windproof cloak

KOLUKA tea leaf

LA milk or butter made from goat's milk; the speaker distinguishes between milk or butter with the accent

LAGA cheese made from goat's milk

LAKALLE a drink made from fermented goat's milk

LAKOLUKA goat's milk (*la*) boiled with *koluka*, a kind of tea leaf

LAROO meat and potato stew

LASSAL market

LON a unit of time in Kanbal; thirty *lon* is about one hour

LOSSO a potato flour dough stuffed with various ingredients and deep fried

LUISHA a luminous blue gem that glows in the dark; extremely precious

LYOKUHAKU a precious milky green stone

NAL a copper coin used in Kanbal; one hundred ten *nal* are worth one silver Yogo coin

NYOKKI a tree root that refreshes the mouth when chewed; the Herders often chew on it

SANGA a yaklike animal that lives on the mountain plateaus of Kanbal

SHIRUYA a type of blanket used in New Yogo

SOOTEE LAN Rider of the Water Currents; a highly intelligent water creature

TITI LAN The Ermine Riders; a little people who live in the caves by day and hunt at night; legend claims that anyone who hinders their hunting will go crazy

TOGAL a poison made from a plant; the Herders use it to fight eagles; a small amount applied to the eyelids dilates the pupils allowing the user to see in the dark

TOH KAL the Titi Lan word for the Herders, it means "Big Brother"; the Herders call the Titi Lan "Chil Kal" or "Little Brother"

YORAM the thunder god and creator in Kanbalese mythology

YUKKA a sweet, tangy fruit

YUKKAL a plant; the juice of its leaves raises body temperature

This book was edited by Cheryl Klein and designed by Phil Falco. The text was set in Adobe Garamond Pro, a typeface designed by Robert Slimbach in 1989. The display type was set in Bureau Eagle, designed by David Berlow in 1990. The book was typeset at NK Graphics and printed and bound at R. R. Donnelley in Crawfordsville, Indiana. The production was supervised by Susan Jeffers Casel. The manufacturing was supervised by Jess White.